Richard S. Ferguson

Early Cumberland and Westmorland Friends

Anatiposi

Richard S. Ferguson

Early Cumberland and Westmorland Friends

Reprint of the original.

1st Edition 2023 | ISBN: 978-3-38210-033-9

Anatiposi Verlag is an imprint of Outlook Verlagsgesellschaft mbH.

Verlag (Publisher): Outlook Verlag GmbH, Zeilweg 44, 60439 Frankfurt, Deutschland
Vertretungsberechtigt (Authorized to represent): E. Roepke, Zeilweg 44, 60439 Frankfurt, Deutschland
Druck (Print): Books on Demand GmbH, In de Tarpen 42, 22848 Norderstedt, Deutschland

EARLY

CUMBERLAND AND WESTMORLAND FRIENDS

A SERIES OF BIOGRAPHICAL SKETCHES OF EARLY MEMBERS OF THE SOCIETY OF FRIENDS IN THOSE COUNTIES.

BY

RICHARD S. FERGUSON, M.A.,

BARRISTER-AT-LAW.

LONDON:
F. BOWYER KITTO, 5, BISHOPSGATE WITHOUT.

CARLISLE: CHAS. THURNAM AND SONS.

1871.

PREFACE.

ABOUT one half of the following biographical Sketches appeared, at various intervals, in the columns of the *Carlisle Journal*. Some readers may be surprised that the author, who is not a member of the Society of Friends, should have selected such a subject. It was in part accidental. The author was searching for books illustrative of Cumberland and Westmorland manners and customs, when he hit by accident upon extracts from the Journal of Thomas Story. This induced inquiries, which have ended in the production of this volume, the purpose whereof is explained at the end of the Biographical accounts; and the Appendix will be found to contain a record of the sufferings of [illegible]nds in these counties, for the

TO

JOSEPH PEASE, Esq.,

LATE M.P. FOR SOUTH DURHAM,

AS A SLIGHT TOKEN OF GRATITUDE

FOR

THE KIND INTEREST HE HAS TAKEN

IN

THIS LITTLE BOOK.

PREFACE.

ABOUT one half of the following biographical Sketches appeared, at various intervals, in the columns of the *Carlisle Journal*. Some readers may be surprised that the author, who is not a member of the Society of Friends, should have selected such a subject. It was in part accidental. The author was searching for books illustrative of Cumberland and Westmorland manners and customs, when he hit by accident upon extracts from the Journal of Thomas Story. This induced inquiries, which have ended in the production of this volume, the purpose whereof is explained at the end of the Biographical accounts; and the Appendix will be found to contain a record of the suff the early Friends in these counties staunchness of their advocacy of civil and religious liberty, and for their opposition to all Ecclesiastical claims.

The author has to thank many gentlemen for friendly guidance through paths of literature before unknown to him. To Mr. John Hallam, of Bishop Auckland, and to Mr. Hudson Scott, of Carlisle, his best thanks are due for much friendly criticism, advice, and information; while to the latter gentleman he is indebted for the supervision of the press, a task which a tour abroad, compulsorily taken in search of health, prevented the author from undertaking. The author is also indebted to Mr. J. B. Braithwaite, of Lincoln's Inn; Mrs. Head, of Rickerby; the late Mr. Crosfield, of Ambleside; Mr. G. G. Mounsey, of Castletown; Mr. Jackson, of Fleatham House, Saint Bees; Mr. W. N. Hodgson, M.P.; and many others, for loans, or proffered loans, of books, and for kind introductions. He has also to thank Mr. Joseph Smith, the compiler of that most valuable work, which no historical library should be without, "A Descriptive Catalogue of Friends' Books." The early literature of the Society of Friends is little known, but contains most valuable information as to the manners and customs of England, Scotland, Ireland, and America, in the seventeenth and eighteenth centuries. Through the intricacies of this literature no one can find his way without the aid of Mr. Smith's most exhaustive book. To the author, Mr. Smith showed great kindness, both by the loan of books, and by personally assisting him to search through the Library of the Society of Friends, in Bishopsgate, London.

To Mr. Joseph Pease, the author owes a great debt of gratitude for the interest he has taken in this book, and for very kind wishes conveyed to him through Mr. J. B. Braithwaite.

INDEX.

EARLY CUMBERLAND AND WESTMORLAND FRIENDS.

If ever the history of great religious revivals is fully written, a curious connection will be found to exist between wild and mountainous scenery and certain forms of religious enthusiasm. Instances will readily occur to our readers, but their thoughts will be apt to travel for examples to the continent rather than to direct themselves towards the counties of Cumberland and Westmorland, or to associate familiar localities with religious persecutions, and a missionary enthusiasm, which sent forth its messengers far beyond the limits of the British Isles, to Holland, to Germany, and even to America and the West Indies. Nowhere did George Fox, the founder of the Society of Friends, more readily find disciples than among the dalesmen of Cumberland and Westmorland: the number of his followers there, the boldness of their

away before they could be called to account, but Besse, in two huge folio volumes, has published in minute details the memoranda thus kept.

In the Williamson correspondence, we find the Quaker postmasters at Appleby and Burgh accused of opening the letters of Royalists; we find the famous "Kipper Rigg Plot" imputed by Sir Philip Musgrave to the Quakers, and Sir Philip under the belief that they intended to cut his throat as the commencement of the rising. The object of this plot, which was betrayed and so failed, was "to force the King to perform his promises made at Breda, grant liberty of conscience to all but Romanists, take away excise, chimney money, and all taxes whatsoever, and restore a Gospel magistracy and mercy." To us it seems certain that Sir Philip and the local magistracy lumped all Nonconformists together under the comprehensive name of "fanatics" or "Quakers," and that thus much is laid in the Williamson Papers to the account of the Society of Friends, which should rather have been put down to other societies of the day, more concerned in political struggles, and more apt to attempt to redress their wrongs by the sword. The "Kipper Rigg Plot" was certainly at the time imputed to the Society, and George Whitehead himself was brought to Whitehall from the prison, where he was confined on a charge of illegal preaching, and examined as to his complicity in the plot: no grounds, however, appearing for suspecting him, the matter was let drop. The chief leader of the plot was one Captain Atkinson of Mallerstang, who was certainly not a member of the Society of Friends; but among his subordinates were some who had long been disowned by the Society; hence, perhaps, arose the idea that the plot was of the Society's making. Another circumstance would strengthen this: Atkinson, when hotly pursued by the Musgraves, surrendered himself into the hands of Thomas Braithwaite, of Burnside, and Braithwaite, of Warcop: these two concealed the surrender from the other local magistrates, and carried Atkinson off to York, where they hoped to find the Duke of Buckingham: not succeeding in this, the three returned to Appleby, and thence started to London: on the road Atkinson escaped on a horse belonging to one of the Braithwaites. As the Braithwaites were then or shortly afterwards Friends, all this tended to apparently connect the Society with Atkinson's plot; whereas their motive was, we fancy, the humane one of procuring for Atkinson a fair trial for his life, for Sir Philip Musgrave and Sir Thomas Gower, the Sheriff of York, intended to hang him, as soon as they caught him, dealing with him under martial law, they being in arms at the head of the *posse comitatus*, which was called out to repress his insurrection.

The place and the date at which the Society of Friends took root in the two counties can be given precisely, though a few scattered converts may have been made before; and it is doubtful whether James Nayler's visit to Westmorland preceded or followed that of Fox: we fancy it followed very closely. Nayler's visit is narrated by Besse, and to the extracts from that work given in our Appendix our readers should refer. Burn and Nicholson, in their History of Westmorland, give the following account of the local origin of the Society:—

"In the time of Oliver Cromwell, Francis Higginson appears to have been vicar of Kirkby Stephen. He was very active against the Quakers, who sprang up at that time; and writ two very notable pamphlets against them.

"As these discourses of Mr. Higginson are extremely scarce (for we have not found more than one printed copy thereof), it may not be amiss to preserve some of the contents of the same.

"From these it appears that the Quakers, at their first setting forward, committed various kinds of extravagances and disorders; which, probably, if they had not been opposed, would more readily have subsided. But the ministers, justices of the peace, constables, and others, followed these people about, disputed with them, bound them over to the peace, procured them to be indicted, and by such opposition rendered the sect considerable.

"Mr. Higginson produceth instances of these people running about the streets, foaming and bellowing out such like expressions as these: 'Repent, repent! Wo, wo! 'The Judge of the world is come!' Some of them stood naked upon the market cross, on the market days, preaching from thence to the people. Particularly, he mentions the wife of one Edmund Adlington, of Kendal, who went naked through the streets there; and two others of the Society, a man and a woman, who called themselves Adam and Eve, went publicly naked, and when examined concerning the same at the assizes, the man affirmed that the power of God was upon him, and he was commanded so to do.

"Many of them in their assemblies, sometimes men, but more frequently women and children, or they who had long fasted, would fall down suddenly, as in an epileptic fit, and there lie grovelling upon the ground, struggling as it were for life, and sometimes more quietly as if they were just expiring. Whilst the agony of the fit was upon them, they would foam at the mouth, their lips would quiver, their flesh and joints would tremble, and their bellies swell like a blown bladder. In such fit they continued sometimes an hour or two; and when it left them they roared out with a voice loud and horrible.

"All which easily accounts for the name of Quakers being given to them."

Now, it must be noted, that this is taken from the accounts written by Francis Higginson, who was an opponent of the Society, and a constant instigator of the local magistracy to severity against them: it must therefore be taken *cum grano.* It repeats calumnies against the Society which have been long since exploded, and it gives an origin for the word "Quaker" at variance with the received one, that it was bestowed on Fox by a justice at Derby. In point of date, too, it appears to be prior to either Fox's or Nayler's visits to Westmorland: hence we fancy that Higginson had been waging war against some religious revivalists raised up by the strange excitement on religion that prevailed in the days of the Commonwealth. These people, probably poor and ignorant, and without any very formed religious doctrines, would probably be attracted by and become followers of Fox and Nayler, when they visited Westmorland, and thus Fox and Nayler would get credited by Higginson and others with absurdities they knew nothing of. The phenomena he describes might be paralleled by instances taken from religious revivals in very recent years. So little credence do we attach to Higginson's account, that we should not have noticed it but for the fact that Burn and Nicholson have done so; and in writing on Westmorland history, we could not well overlook anything advanced by them.

The better account, and that which is substantiated by the authorities is, that, in 1652, while George Fox was travelling in the Yorkshire dales, he visited the annual fair held for hiring servants at Sedbergh, where he preached in the church yard; a disturbance took place, an attempt was made to put him down, and one Francis Howgill, an Independent minister, took part with Fox, and procured him a hearing. Next Sunday, Francis Howgill and one John Audland, also an Independent minister, and both afterwards energetic ministers among the Friends, were preaching in Firbank Chapel, in Westmorland. To this place came George Fox, and, in the afternoon, after people had had their dinners, he addressed a congregation of about a thousand people from a rock which was close to the chapel, so close, indeed, that many of the old people listened to him from the chapel windows; while he explained to them that he preached from the rock rather than in the chapel, because, in his opinion, no more sanctity appertained to the one than to the other. The result of this meeting at Firbank, famous in the annals of the Society of Friends, was that he obtained many followers, including both Howgill and Audland and others, who became the earliest and most ardent missionaries of the Society. From Firbank, Fox proceeded by Preston Patrick to Kendal, where he held a meeting in the Town Hall. He records that one of his hearers, named Cock, afterwards met him in the street, and pressed on his acceptance a roll of tobacco, which, however, Fox refused. He next went to Underbarrow and Crook, at which places he had great success. He then returned to Lancashire, but frequently during the year visited Westmorland. From Westmorland and North Lancashire he collected the first missionaries of the Society, namely, Edward Burrough, John Audland, Francis Howgill, John Camm, George Whitehead, Richard Hubberthorne, Thomas Holmes, Miles Halhead, and Miles Hubbersty, the majority of whom were

Westmorland men. He numbered also among his local followers and friends two men of official position, namely, Gervaise Benson and Anthony Pearson. The first was a justice for Cumberland and Westmorland, and the second for both these counties and for Lancashire as well. Both were on the Bench at Appleby at the trial of James Nayler; both were converted by him, and both afterwards plunged into print. Pearson, who also became a preacher, wrote a book against tithes in 1657, entitled the "Great Case of Tithes,—a Treatise addressed to the Farmers and Husbandmen of England." It developes the history of tithe, its absence from the early Christian Church, its first introduction, and the opposition it met at various eras. Benson started a controversy that lasted some years with Allan Smallwood, D.D., over a sermon which that divine preached in Carlisle Cathedral on the 17th August, 1664, and in which he argued that oaths might be taken on fitting occasions. Benson also wrote a reply to "The Quaker Shaken," by John Gilpin, of Kendal, an apostate Friend.

In the following year, 1653, Fox was informed that the people in Cumberland had vowed to take his life if he put foot in that county. Fox was no way deterred by this, but paid a visit to one Miles Wennington, and then joined Justice Pearson and his wife, who were on their way to

Carlisle Quarter Sessions. Fox only accompanied them as far as Bootle, where he presented himself at church on Sunday, and so soon as the priest had finished preaching, he commenced, according to the custom of the time, a discourse of his own. Two sermons in such rapid succession were more than the people would stand, or else the priest incited them to violence; though it was then usual for any minister of any religious society to preach and officiate in a parish church after the hours of regular service. They pulled Fox out into the churchyard, and, spite of the constable's exertions, beat him severely, nearly breaking his wrist. Nothing daunted by this rough treatment, Fox returned in the afternoon to the churchyard, and seated himself upon a cross there, while some of his companions entered the church, where they found a stranger from London officiating; they beckoned Fox in, and, spite of the priest from London, he succeeded in preaching, being protected by the constable—a proceeding which was so little to the two priests' liking, "that they foamed at the mouth." In the mêlée that took place, before Fox could get a hearing, his coat was cut with a knife, which did not penetrate his doublet. Fox stayed a few days at "Milholm in Bootel," and from thence sent one John Lancaster to make an appointment with priest Wilkinson, who had three churches near Cockermouth, whereof Brigham was one, and Mosser Chapel and Greysouthen probably the other two. At one of Wilkinson's churches (name not given) the concourse of people anxious to hear Fox was so great that the place resembled a fair, and his audience included a party of twelve soldiers and their wives from the Cromwellian garrison of Carlisle, priest Larkham of Cockermouth, and others. Both here and at Brigham Fox had a much more friendly reception than at Bootle; the people welcomed him into the church, where he preached, the effects of which Wilkinson immediately tried to counteract by a sermon of several hours in length. Fox, however, gained the day and convinced many, including the twelve soldiers, who went on with him to Cockermouth, protected him, and interfered with those who wished to prevent him from preaching in the church of that town. Cockermouth must then have been an humble-minded place, for the chief inhabitants tried to get rid of Fox by representing that there were no men in the place learned enough to dispute with him; a put-off which did not answer, for Fox replied that he came not to dispute but to preach, and preach he did, "largely," as his journal expresses it. By Caldbeck and the Borders, Fox passed to Carlisle, where the Baptists and their pastor met him, and held a meeting in the Abbey, from which the Dean had been evicted, and his house let for a manufactory. Fox quaintly enough describes the pastor of the Carlisle Baptists as "an high notionist and a flashy man, who came to me and asked me what must be damned. I was moved immediately to tell him that which spake in him was to be damned; this stopped the pastor's mouth." From the Abbey, Fox went to the Castle; the Cromwellian garrison, probably composed of Puritans and Independents, was at once assembled by tuck of drum to hear him preach: some of the sergeants, however, demurred, not to his preaching, but to his doctrine. On the market day, which during the latter part of the Commonwealth was, by Act of Parliament, held at Carlisle on Friday, Fox preached in the market-place. His journal tells us that "the magistrates had both threatened and sent their sergeants; and the magistrates' wives had said that if I came there they would pluck the hair from off my head, and that the sergeants should take me up." It is curious that in all the earlier records of the Friends, the fair sex—the priests' wives and the magistrates' wives—appear to have been the most bitter against them. Spite of the Carlisle magistrates' wives, and their threats, Fox did preach in the Market-place, and all passed off peaceably. On Sunday he went to the "Steeple House." It is not clear whether this means the Cathedral or St. Cuthbert's Church; but Fox, by this expression in his journal, clearly points at the chief ecclesiastical building in Carlisle, and we may assume it to be the Cathedral. There he attempted to preach. A riot ensued—soldiers, magistrates' wives, and mob, all fighting with sticks and stones, and yelling "Down with the Roundheads!" until at last the Governor of the Castle appeared with several files of musketeers, and cleared the place, and arrested some of the rioters. Fox escaped by connivance of the military. Next day he was brought under a warrant to the Town Hall, before the justices and magistrates of the city, who were all Presbyterians and Independents, but of whom Thomas Craston and Cuthbert Studholm are the only two whose names are preserved. After examining Fox, the justices committed him to prison "as a blasphemer, an heretic, and a seducer." We will take Fox's own account of his imprisonment:—

"The jail at Carlisle has two jailers, an upper and an under, which looked like two great bear-wards. Now, when I was brought in, the upper jailer had me up into a great chamber, and told me that I should have what I would in that room; but I told him he should not expect any money from me, for I would neither lie in any of his beds, nor eat any of his victuals. Then he put me into another room, where, after awhile, I got something to lie upon. There I lay until the assizes came, and then all the talk and cry was that I was to be hanged. And the high sheriff, whose name was Wilfrey Lawson, stirred them much up to take away my life, and said he would guard me to my execution himself. They were in a black, dark rage, and set three musketeers for guard upon me, one at my chamber door, another at the stairs foot, and a third at the street door; and none they would let come at me, except one sometimes, to bring me some necessary things. At night they would bring up priests to me, sometimes as late as the tenth hour in the night, and they would be exceeding rude and devilish. Great ladies also (as they were called) came to see the man that was to die."

The "great ladies" were doomed to be disappointed, for the clerk of assize, or the clerk to the justices, discovered a legal flaw in the mittimus under which Fox was committed, and he was not put upon his trial at the assizes, but was left in confinement so close that neither Benson nor Pearson, justices though they were, could get permission to visit him.

"The next day," Fox continues, "after the judges were gone out of the town, an order was sent to the jailer to put me down in the dungeon amongst the mosstroopers, thieves, and murderers, which accordingly he did. A filthy, nasty place it was, where men and women were put together in a very uncivil manner, and never a house of office to it; and the prisoners so lousy that one woman was almost eaten to death with lice. Yet, bad as the place was, the prisoners were all made very loving and subject to me; and some of them were convinced of the truth, as the publicans and harlots were of old; so that they were able to confound a priest, that might come to the grates to dispute. But the jailer was very cruel, and the under-jailer very abusive to me and to the Friends that came to see me; for he would beat Friends with a cudgel that did but come to the window to look in upon me. I could get up to the grate, where sometimes I took in my meat, at which the jailer was often offended. One time he came in a great rage, and fell a beating me with a cudgel, though I was not at the grate at the time; and as he beat me, he cried 'come out of the window,' though I was then far enough from it. Now, while he struck me, I was made to sing in the Lord's power, and that made him rage the more. Then he went and fetched a fiddler, and brought him in where I was, and set him to play, thinking to vex me thereby; but while he played I was moved in the everlasting power of the Lord God to sing; and my voice drowned the noise of the fiddle and struck and confounded them, and made them give over fiddling and go their ways."

Probably, in order to protect Fox, Mrs. Benson, wife of the justice of that name, made it a practice to come to the prison window and take her meals there with Fox. Meanwhile her husband and Pearson strenuously moved to get Fox set free; at their instigation the Parliament (the "Little Parliament") took up the matter, and sent to inquire about the treatment Fox met with, and which both he, Benson, and Pearson, made widely known in letters and broadsheets addressed to the justices and others. This agitation wrought Fox's release, and his gaolers suffered punishment. The upper one was bound over to good behaviour, and the under one put in Fox's place with the moss-troopers. On being set free, Fox went to Caldbeck, where the people beat his comrades severely, nearly killing one, who was a Baptist teacher, with his own sword. Robert Withers, a Friend, one of the party, was arrested by order of Justice Brisco, of Crofton, a Parliamentary colonel and M.P. for Carlisle. Withers was brought before the justice at the house of one Priest Nichols, and Brisco signed and delivered to the constable a warrant for committal to Carlisle gaol. He then asked Withers by what authority he came to bewitch and seduce people. "Robert answered" (see Sewell's History): "'I came not to seduce and bewitch people, but I came in that power which shall make all the powers of the earth bend and bow before it, to wit, the mighty power of God.' Whilst Robert was speaking thus, the dread of the Lord seized on the justice, and so struck him that he called for his warrant again and took it out of the constable's hand, suffering Robert about night to go away." From Caldbeck Fox went to Wigton; there the populace formed a guard armed with pitchforks, and would let no Quaker enter the town. From Wigton he went to Gilsland, which he mentions as noted for thieving, and where he was himself taken for a thief and a horse-stealer. Returning from Gilsland he went to Longlands in Uldale parish: there he addressed a meeting of many thousand people. Fox got, in this visit to the two counties, a large number of converts, and several soldiers joined him, who were shortly discharged from the Parliamentary forces because they would not take an oath of allegiance to Cromwell: John Stubbs is mentioned as an instance at Carlisle: he, his wife, and four children, were after the Restoration much oppressed by Sir Daniel Fleming for their religion. This imprisonment of Fox at Carlisle occurred in 1653. Fox's next visit to the two counties was in 1657, when he held meetings in several places, Great Strickland, Gilsland, Longlands, Abbey Holme, and Pardshaw Crag. He luckily evaded a warrant which was out at Kendal for his arrest, and got clear of the town before the constable could run home for the warrant. At another place in Westmorland the crowds that surrounded him while preaching prevented one of the Otways from doing him bodily violence, for Otway kept riding round the meeting with his rapier drawn, and several times attempted to ride in on Fox. At Great Strickland, Fox found that all the county gentry were assembled at a race meeting: he went there and addressed them; they were also admonished by a chief-constable that was present, a proceeding that would strike the county gentry of the present day as abnormal. In 1663, Fox again entered the two counties, and narrowly escaped arrest at the hands of Sir Philip Musgrave and Sir Daniel Fleming, who had come into power after the Restoration.

We have no records of any further visits; but the number of early preachers of his theology that came from Westmorland and Cumberland, and from North Lancashire, and the number of Friends now to be found there, show how deeply his teaching must have taken root. We can adduce from the Williamson papers evidence as to the growth of the Society. In November, 1663, after the Kippar Rigg Plot had been discovered and provided against, Sir Daniel Fleming writes to Secretary Williamson: "If mischief arise now, it will be from non-licensed ministers or from Quakers, of whom there are too many in the part of the county joining to Lancashire, where George Fox and most of his culls have been long kennelled. They keep weekly meetings within eight miles of each other through all this country, if not through England: they will do mischief most resolutely if Fox or any other of their grand speakers dictate it, and some threaten already." Such being Fleming's sentiments, he acted up to them, and in the following January writes to Williamson: "Proceeded smartly at Lancaster assizes against the Quakers; committed George Fox and half-a-score more to close gaol for refusing the oath of allegiance, and fined sixty on the new Act, although Mrs. Fell (Oliver's Judge Fell's widow) did her utmost to prevent it. Many fined at Appleby. This will soon stop their meetings, unless they obtain favour at Whitehall, which would much encourage them." Later, Fleming writes: "Mrs. Fell, Fox's wife, had a greater meeting than ever at her house the Sunday after the Sessions, on purpose to affront authority, for forty of those fined were fined for meeting at her house.

The only way to deal with her will be to tender her the oath, and premunire her. Several justices are cool to commit Quakers, because the judges have either set them at liberty or given them very small fines." Fleming was as good as his word with Fox and Mrs. Fell: he got the Lancashire Sheriff and Deputy-Lieutenant to tender them the oath, and then persuaded Judge Twysden to commit them both.

Fox afterwards visited America; but into his life we do not intend to go, as he was not born in either Cumberland or Westmorland. However, in Colquhoun's "Short Sketches of some Notable Lives," we have a very interesting, and in the main a correct estimate of Fox's character, which we quote as an antidote to a very incorrect one given by Lord Macaulay:—

"The truth is, that Fox's character had, like many others, two sides; and the contrast between these is so great that one can hardly believe them to belong to the same man.

"On the one side, we have strange thoughts and words, fanciful imaginations—the illusions of an unlettered mind. But such things are not unusual. Dr. Johnson believed in second sight, in dreams and ghosts; and his case presents to us the credulity of a child with the intellect of a giant. But if we turn to the other side of Fox's character, we find this man of fancies and visions confronted with controversialists, Jesuits, and lawyers—puzzling them with his subtlety, and with his logic beating down their fancies. Now, in a court of justice, he confronts the judge, defies the bar, picks flaws in their indictment, quotes against them adverse statutes, and wrings from baffled judges a reluctant acquittal. Then he is in the Protector's court, to meet a man hard to dupe. There he plants himself, his hat on his head, at Oliver's dressing-table; engages him in long discourse; sets before him his duty; presses on him the policy of toleration; till the iron-hearted soldier, first surprised, then attentive, at length interested, extends his hand to the Quaker, bids him repeat his visit, and tells him if they could meet oftener they would be firmer friends. No less remarkable are his courage and skill. As storms thicken, he is always in front of the battle; wherever the strife is vehement, there he is, now in Lancashire, now in Leicester, in Westmorland, or Cornwall; meeting magistrates and judges, braving at Quarter Sessions, vanquishing officers, governors of castles, and judges. Then he sits down calmly to organise, with a forecast equal to that of Wesley, the scheme of Quaker polity, which has lasted to our times. And if we smile at the oddity of his language, at the curious missives which he hurls at mayors and magistrates, gaolers and judges, we find at times a caustic style worthy of Hudibras or Cobbett, in which he lashes the frippery of the Court, or meets the casuistry of the Jesuits or Ultra-Calvinists; and, as we dwell on the words of wisdom in which he tells us of his faith, and cheers the drooping heart of Cromwell's daughter, we perceive that he is no common man, but one who, with a strange training and singular notions, rose by the strength of genius and piety to a wide command over men."

We add two other extracts about Fox: the first is from Sir James Mackintosh. He says of Fox's journal:—

"It is one of the most extraordinary and interesting biographies ever penned, which no reader of competent judgment can peruse without revering the virtue of the man."

Coleridge, in his "Biographia Literaria," writes:—

"There exist folios on the human understanding and on the nature of man, which would have a far juster claim to their high rank and celebrity, if in the whole huge volume they contained as much fulness of heart and intellect as beams forth in many a single page of George Fox."

We have quoted these passages as a set-off against a prejudiced account given of the man by Lord Macaulay.

Fox died in London, in 1690.

Having thus run through Fox's visits to the two counties, we now commence with the proper object of this book, a sketch of those Cumberland and Westmorland worthies who enlisted under his banner, and went forth as missionaries; and first, of Francis Howgill, his protector at Sedbergh Fair.

FRANCIS HOWGILL.

Francis Howgill, of Todthorne, near Grayrigg, was a Westmorland man, educated at one of the universities, and became a minister of the Church of England; but being dissatisfied with its doctrines, he became first an Independent preacher, and afterwards an Anabaptist. In 1652 he met George Fox at Sedbergh fair, where Fox was preaching in the church yard. In the controversy that followed Fox's discourse, Howgill took part and sided with Fox, advocating that he should have a fair hearing. On the Sunday following, Howgill preached in the chapel at Firbank, in Westmorland, to a crowded audience, but delivered only a short sermon, having a vivid presentiment in his mind that Fox would come and preach there. Fox did come, declined to use Howgill's pulpit, but preached for three hours from a rock near the chapel, to an audience of over a thousand people. Francis Howgill and John Audland, also an Independent preacher, were both convinced, and, in pursuance of their convictions, returned the money they had received for preaching, to the parish of Bolton in Lancashire. The priests and magistrates, with whom Howgill had been popular, were much disgusted at his conversion, and put him to prison. "He was locked up in a nasty place at Appleby, in Westmorland, and kept there a prisoner for some time." He afterwards, in 1654, accompanied Justice Pearson, and Edward Burrough to London, and also to Ireland and Bristol, and was one of the first preachers of this Society in London, and officiated at the very first meeting the Society ever held there; it took place at the house of one Robert Dring, in Watling Street. Like Burrough, to whom we shall come presently, he also addressed letters to Oliver Cromwell, complaining of the treatment to which members of the Society were subjected. Little is known of Howgill's doings between 1656 and 1663; but he was travelling in the south of England as a preacher, and at Bristol, which he visited in company with John Camm, his preaching was the occasion of great riots. On returning to his own neighbourhood, in 1663, while in the Market-place of Kendal, he was summoned to appear before the justices, who were holding a court in a tavern. They tendered him the oath of allegiance; and, as he refused to take it, they committed him to Appleby gaol. At Appleby, the judges of assize also tendered him the same oath, and ordered him to be indicted at the next assizes, but offered to release him meanwhile on his giving bond for good behaviour: this he refused to do. During this imprisonment a curious incident happened. Howgill was allowed by the magistrates to go home to Grayrigg, on private affairs, for a few days. He called on Justice Duckett, of Grayrigg Hall, who expressed surprise at seeing him. "What is your will now, Francis? I thought you had been in Appleby gaol." "No, I am not; but I have come with a message from the Lord. Thou hast persecuted the Lord's people; but His hand is now against thee, and He will send a blast upon all that thou hast; and thy name shall rot out of the earth; and this thy dwelling shall become desolate, and an habitation for owls and jackdaws." This prediction was fulfilled. All Duckett's children died without issue, and his daughter begged her bread from door to door. Grayrigg Hall was dismantled by the Lowthers, and was, in 1770, a total ruin. A farm house has now been built on its site.

At the Appleby assizes, in March, Howgill appeared before Judges Twysden and Turner, who were supported on the bench by Sir Philip Musgrave, Sir Daniel Fleming, and Sir John Lowther. Musgrave appears to have been the great instigator of the proceedings against Howgill; while Fleming, who was one of the great lawyers of his day, had come prepared with an indictment ready drawn against him for holding illegal meetings.

The two judges were anxious to deal mildly with the prisoner, and would have let him go untried, if he would only enter into a bond for his good behaviour; this he declined, though the judges pressed him much, and gave him to the end of the assizes to consider. Musgrave, Fleming, (so severe a persecutor of Friends that one who died at Lancaster was carried round the country with an inscription on his coffin, "Persecuted by Daniel Fleming until death,") and Lowther, urged severity; but the judges, with a moderation which Howgill, in his defence, admitted, were very loth to commit him back to prison: finally, they were overruled, and did so, leaving him untried until next August. The justices, thus baffled in their wish to get a heavy sentence passed on him, kept him in solitary confinement, and no one got speech of him, except without the gaoler's knowledge. In August, Judge Turner attended the assizes again, and Howgill was put on his trial. The judge appears to have been as anxious as possible to have dealt mercifully with him; but the prisoner would not yield at all to laws which he deemed unrighteous. He was found guilty of refusing the oath of allegiance; and the judge, in a voice so low that it could scarcely be heard, sentenced him thus:—"You are put out of the King's protection and the benefit of the law; your lands are confiscated to the King during your life, and your goods and chattels for ever, and you to be prisoner during your life." Even after passing sentence, the judge held out strong hopes of mercy; but Howgill would not make the slightest concession to obtain it, and so his sentence was carried out. During his imprisonment he wrote several things, particularly a treatise against oaths. He died in Appleby gaol, in 1668, after an imprisonment of about five years. He was married, and left a son and several daughters, to the youngest of whom, Abigail, he wrote from Appleby gaol a long letter of advice and counsel, which is to be found in Sewell's History of the Friends. Howgill was accompanied on some of his travels by Edward Burrough.

EDWARD BURROUGH.

Edward Burrough was born in the barony of Kendal, in Westmorland, about 1634. His parents were people of honest and virtuous life, and, in religion, Episcopalians. They gave their son the best education they could get for him in the barony, and though he was not skilful in languages, yet he "had the tongue of the learned, and in his public ministry was very fluent and elegant in speech, even according to the judgment of learned men." As a mere child he appears to have been precocious and grave beyond his years, averse to the ordinary pleasures of youth, and fond of religious conversation and society. He was remarkably well versed in Holy Scripture, and is said to have been "in youth endued with wisdom above his equals in years." He was, by his parents, brought up to the Episcopal worship, but at the early age of twelve he began to frequent the meetings of the Presbyterians, and shortly afterwards joined that body, although he was reviled for it by his friends and acquaintances. A Presbyterian he remained until he was seventeen, when he began to be troubled much with religious doubts. On one occasion, while praying, he seemed to hear a voice, saying "thou art ignorant of God, thou knowest not where He is, nor what He is; to what purpose is thy prayer?" From this time he grew more and more ascetic; he took upon him to rebuke others for vain conversation and wickedness, and grew weary of hearing the priests. While in this condition, he heard George Fox preach at Underbarrow or Crook, and afterwards conversed with him. The enthusiasm of that remarkable man communicated itself to Burrough. He was convinced, and became one of Fox's followers. For this he was rejected by his relations and turned out of doors by his father; his profession of Quakerism subjected him to much suffering, and it is recorded that not only was he reviled and slandered, but actually caned, buffeted, and imprisoned.

In 1654, when Burrough was nineteen, he went up to London as a preacher in company with Francis Howgill, and with Anthony Pearson, who, as we have before mentioned, had formerly been a Justice of the Peace of Cumberland, Westmorland, and Lancashire, hot in the persecution of Friends, but who had been convinced, and had written a book against tithes. Howgill and Pearson held, as we have said in our account of Howgill, the first Friends' meeting that had ever been held in London. Burrough was not present, but appears to have been preaching elsewhere on that day. He and Howgill were however the first preachers of the Society that systematically preached in London on every opportunity. On one occasion, Burrough was passing a place where some of the Londoners were spending their evening in wrestling. He joined the spectators (he was a Westmorland man), and saw one stalwart champion throw three opponents in succession. No one was bold enough to enter the ring with this hero, and so Burrough went in and presented himself; "and having looked upon the wrestler with a serious countenance," the man was not a little surprised, instead of an airy antagonist, to meet with "a grave and awful young man." Burrough, however, did not mean wrestling, but preaching, and his surprised audience proved a very attentive one.

Historians have noticed that the early Friends and the Roman Catholics were oppressed and distrained by the same penal and test laws; hence partially arose a notion that the two were connected, and we find that the early Friends were often supposed to be Jesuits in disguise. Burrough, extending his travels to Bristol, fell under similar suspicion, as the following curious warrant issued by the local magistracy shows:—

"City of Bristol.

"To the constables of the peace of the ward of ———, and to every of them. Forasmuch as information hath been given us upon oath, that certain persons of the Franciscan order in Rome have of late come over into England, and, under the notion of Quakers, drawn together several multitudes of people in London; and whereas certain strangers, going under the names of John Camm, John Audland, George Fox, James Naylor, Francis Howgill, and Edward Burrough, and others unknown, have lately resorted to this city, and in like manner, under the notion of Quakers, drawn multitudes of people after them, and occasioned very great disturbances amongst us; and forasmuch as by the said information it appeareth to us to be very probable, and much to be suspected, that the said persons so lately come hither are some of those that came from Rome as aforesaid."

Then follows an order for their arrest, and this warrant is signed by the Mayor of Bristol and several aldermen. In the following year, 1665, Burrough and Howgill went to Ireland, from whence they were, after a stay of six months, expelled by Henry Cromwell, the Lord Deputy of Ireland. They made a convert during their stay of one William Ames, a Baptist teacher, and military officer—a strict disciplinarian, who, if any soldier under his colours had been guilty of any immorality on a Sunday, tied the delinquent up for punishment by his neck and his heels. Nor was he the only man of military rank whom Burrough converted in Ireland: Colonel Phare, and many, of similar rank, became Friends: and also Cornet Cooke, of Cromwell's own troop of horse. Burrough afterwards travelled as far as Dunkirk, then held by the English, for the purpose of disputing with the Jesuits there; but they were no willing hearers. The rest of his life he spent in London, as a preacher, visiting occasionally Bristol and other places. He addressed, at various times, to Oliver Cromwell several very plain-spoken epistles of great length, in which he rebuked the Protector, "because he had not been faithful in God's work; but that he had taken his rest and ease upon a lofty mountain of pride and vain-glory, having set up himself to be worshipped, and exalting his own horn."

These letters were occasioned by the fact that Cromwell allowed the Friends to be persecuted; and, in the very plainest language, Burrough points out to him that by winking at such doings he was falsifying promises he had given, before the days of his prosperity. When Cromwell died, Burrough, by accident, fell in with his state-funeral, and was so disgusted with the "sinful idolatry of it," that he printed an address in which he found unsparing fault with the whole ceremony:—

"Alas for him, who was once a great instrument in the hand of the Lord to break down many idolatrous images! Did not the Lord once stir up his heart against all such things? and did not once his children, officers, soldiers, and army, pull down all the images and crosses, and all such popish stuff, whenever they met with it? What grievous and abominable stuff is this? Have they now made a costly image of him? And are such as were once his soldiers now guarding it and watching over it, and his children and officers following it, and multitudes of the inhabitants of London wondering and gazing at an image of him? This is sad, and a great pity. What a change is this in so short a time!"

In addition to his letters to Cromwell, he addressed others to Richard Cromwell, and to Richard's Parliament, exhorting them to desist from all persecution for religion.

When Charles II. was restored, the Society of Friends ceased, for a brief time, to suffer persecution in England. Indeed, the new Government appears rather to have courted them. A paper of queries, said to have been drawn up by Edward, Earl of Clarendon, was circulated among them, with a view to ascertaining their sentiments about the Restoration. Burrough answered the queries, speaking out very freely, but declaring sentiments favourable to the Restoration, and finishing with a bold exhortation to the King to fear and reverence the Lord. Though persecution was stayed for a short time in England, yet it went on in New England, with more severity than ever. Burrough sought an interview with Charles II., and told him that there was "a vein of innocent blood opened in his dominions, that, if not stopped, would overrun all." The King replied that he would stop it, and signed a mandamus at once; and, at Burrough's request, nominated one Samuel Shattock, a Friend who had been banished from New England, on pain of death if ever he returned there, to take the warrant. Burrough must have had great weight with the King, for, besides expediting the warrant and entrusting it to Shattock, he allowed the Society, for greater speed, to send it out in one of their own ships.

The insurrection of the Fifth Monarchy men after the Restoration, drew from the Government a proclamation against Fifth Monarchy men and Quakers; and then commenced the hottest period of persecutions that the Society has ever undergone. In 1662, Burrough was arrested while preaching at a meeting in London, held at the Bull and Mouth, and committed to Newgate by Mr. Alderman Richard Brown. He was tried at the Old Bailey Sessions, fined twenty marks, and sent to prison, as he would not pay. After eight months' imprisonment, he died of gaol fever, the natural result of the close packing he underwent; for the prisoners slept in hammocks, three tiers one above the other, a layer of beds being on the floor below. The King, on hearing of Burrough's imprisonment, sent a special order for his release, which Alderman Brown contrived to burke; and the careless monarch probably never inquired whether his order had been obeyed. Burrough was only twenty-eight when he died. His death was much mourned by the Society of Friends, and George Fox issued a short address to the Society, to calm their minds, an honour he never did to any other Friend in like case, however eminent.

He appears to have been a man of great boldness and vigour, who preached in forcible language, and was, as Sewell, in his History of Friends, says, called, "not unjustly, a son of thunder. . . . To thunder against sin and iniquity was his peculiar talent; inasmuch that once, preaching very zealously in meeting, and perceiving there were some contrite souls that wanted spiritually refreshing food, he was heard to intimate that, though his present speaking was not milk for babes, yet he would remember such anon, and administer to them also; but at present he must thresh the whore."

Burrough's writings, mostly controversial, form a folio volume of 829 pages; Richard Baxter and John Bunyan are among the number of his opponents. He was remarkable for his addresses to the ruling powers of his time, of whose proneness to persecution, and the evil consequences resulting from it, he faithfully warned them. Many of his expressions may be considered as predicting the downfall of the Government which supported it: and his views of civil and religious liberty, as combined with that duty of Christian subjection, which we owe to the Government under which we live, are stated by him in clear and strong language, in several of his publications. One of Burrough's companions at Bristol was John Audland, and with him we will deal next.

JOHN AUDLAND, AND ANN AUDLAND, AFTERWARDS CAMM.

John Audland was born in 1630, near Kendal, of respectable parents, and though at first disposed to youthful amusements, became, when about seventeen, religiously inclined, and being "mighty in the Scriptures," became an eminent teacher in a society which was separated from the national way of worship: he often, however, preached in the churches in his neighbourhood. During the Commonwealth, it was, as we have remarked before, not unusual for dissenters to occupy the parish pulpits, when the parish parson did not require them, or had finished his sermon, a fact which made the appearances of Fox and his followers in "steeple houses" less strange than they seem to us of the present day. Audland was at the famous meeting at Firbank Chapel, and to his house George Fox went after he had concluded his discourse, and Audland was added to the number of Fox's followers and missionaries. He travelled as a preacher generally with John Camm, who was his most intimate friend, and with him visited Bristol and London. Like Camm, he died of consumption, induced by his missionary exertions, particularly in addressing large open-air meetings at Bristol, the scene of most of his labours and of his persecutions. His death occurred in 1663; he was buried at Birkrigg Park, where his friend Camm had been interred some six years before. Audland did not publish much; his printed works consist of Epistles to his Friends, and one or two controversial pieces. He was a man of a very amiable disposition, and of comely person.

His wife was Ann Newby, daughter of Richard Newby, of Kendal. She was a well-educated woman, and married John Audland in 1650, when he was about twenty, and she was a little older. She was convinced at the same time as her husband, and joined him in preaching, for which she was, in 1653, committed to prison at Bishop's Auckland, where she addressed the people from the prison window. She was afterwards put on her trial for blasphemy at Banbury, in Oxfordshire. The presiding Judge tried hard to acquit her, but the magistrates had biassed the jury, who brought in a verdict of guilty, which the Judge upset as bad in law. She was, however, sent to prison, because she would not give bail for her good behaviour, and was confined at Banbury for eight months, in a place underground, hard by the common sewer, and infested with toads and frogs. Two years after the death of her first husband, she married Thomas Camm, son of her husband's friend, John Camm. Her second husband was imprisoned, on account of his religious opinions, for three years, at Kendal; and for six at Appleby. She died near Kendal in 1705, aged 78. Although a preacher herself, she rather disapproved of her sex in that capacity, and would scarcely preach at large meetings, if any qualified man was present.

JOHN CAMM.

In connection with Howgill, Audland, and Burrough, we have mentioned the name of JOHN CAMM, of Camsgil. He was a member of a good and substantial family, which had long possessed a seat at Camsgil, a place in the barony of Westmorland, which took its name from its owners. From his childhood he was religiously inclined, and, with several others, had separated from the national Church, and was wont to worship apart. He was also present at the great meeting at Firbank Chapel, and to it he owed his convincement. He was one of the band of missionary Friends whose zeal was first kindled by Fox's discourse at that meeting. To devote himself to missionary efforts, he gave up great prospects in life, for he was, as his son tells us, "a man of wealth, and rising rapidly in the world." His first journeys were in the north of England and Scotland; in 1654 he went south with Francis Howgill, on purpose to "declare the message of the Lord to Oliver Cromwell, then called Protector." Oliver Cromwell received the two graciously, but misconceived their object, and supposed that they wished him to compel people to be religious by law. To correct this misapprehension, Camm wrote to him, cautioning him also against countenancing oppression, and ending with these words: "Take heed, for he that is in high places is subject to many temptations." From London Camm travelled to Bristol with John Audland, his intimate friend, at which place their visits occasioned much rioting; they were taken for emissaries of the Pope, and ill-treated. Camm returned, in 1656, to his home at Preston Patrick, in Westmorland, a very infirm man, and died there, aged 52. Some accounts say his death occurred in 1656, others in 1665. As he predeceased John Audland by six years, 1656 or 1657 must be the correct date. He was buried at Birkrigg.

John Camm left a family. His son, Thomas Camm, married the widow of John Audland, and was a minister, whose imprisonments we have mentioned in our account of his wife.

GEORGE WHITEHEAD.

Continuing with these early Westmorland Friends, whom we have mentioned as among Fox's earliest missionaries, we now come to George Whitehead, of Orton.

The most famous of all the early missionaries of Quakerism was George Whitehead, of Orton. He is, after George Fox, the chief founder of the Society; and, both from the great age he attained, and the lead he took in the Society's business, may be deemed, to a great extent, its father.

He was born at Orton, in Westmorland, about the year 1635, and was educated at the free school at Blencoe, in Cumberland, where, as he tells us, he "loved retirement, with some other sober, studious scholars, though but mean and poor in the world, rather than the company of loose, extravagant boys, though of the gentry, or richer sort, who were given to much play and gaming." He afterwards kept a school at Orton, and was an attendant at Orton Church. At the early age of fourteen, Whitehead conceived objections, on religious grounds, to the promiscuous singing of

David's Psalms in church. He was also shocked because the priests did not practise what they preached. These reasons, operating upon his mind, led him to attend Quaker meetings held at Sunnyside, near Greyrigg, at the house of a Captain Ward. On one occasion, he was, he says, deeply affected, more than by any preaching he ever heard, by seeing a young maid go out of the meeting, and fling herself face downwards on the ground, crying out, "Lord, what shall I do to be clean?" At one of these meetings, some time in the year 1652, Whitehead met George Fox, and, fired by his enthusiasm, became one of his earliest missionaries. Whitehead's first journey was taken in 1653 or 1654, and was to Norfolk and Suffolk. At Warwick he was put into prison, where Hunt, the gaoler, demanded from three of them fourpence apiece per night for one bed for the lot. Rather than pay this, they slept for eight weeks on the bare boards of the floor, it being winter, and a cold one. At the city sessions, Whitehead, and his companions in prison, were brought before Recorder Cook, by whom they were discharged, but were detained by Hunt for fees. Hunt dying soon, they got their liberty, through the pity of his widow. After his release, Whitehead continued in the same neighbourhood, often being mobbed and persecuted. One one occasion, he was rescued by a trooper, who interfered on his behalf. The trooper afterwards turned a Friend, but it was five-and-twenty years before Whitehead heard of his conversion, or even knew his name, and then they both met as prisoners in Norwich Gaol. Whitehead, and some other Friends, shortly after this first discharge from Norwich Gaol, got into Edmundbury Gaol, Whitehead being committed under a mittimus which called him an "idle, wandering fellow from Westmorland." There they suffered much. The gaoler kept an alehouse, and was also a Presbyterian priest. On Sundays, he expounded to the prisoners; on week-days he and his tapster encouraged them to drink. The Friends would neither pay him fees, nor drink, but ever preached against drunkenness. Incensed by this, the gaoler took away from his prisoners their clothes, even their nightcaps, and put the prisoners themselves into the common ward with burglars, and even into a pit underground, and encouraged drunken felons to kick, strike, and abuse them. After fifteen months' imprisonment, they were released by an order of Oliver Cromwell, procured by the intercession of one Mary Sandars, a waiting gentlewoman in Cromwell's family; Sir Francis Russell was ordered to see the warrant executed. Soon after his release, Whitehead fell into the hands of Justice Surden, one of those who had signed the mittimus for his committal to Bury Gaol. By order of this justice, Whitehead was publicly whipt through Nayland as a vagrant, a piece of flagrant injustice, for he was travelling on his own horse. The constables were also ordered to pass him from place to place. In 1657, Whitehead returned to his parents in Westmorland, who received him joyfully, though the Presbyterian priests had tried to poison their minds against him. While at home, Whitehead attended meetings of Friends in Cumberland and Westmorland. These were usually held on commons and mountainous places. He mentions that, in stormy weather, they generally found that one side or other of Pardsey Crag afforded shelter. He also had a hand in an attempt to establish meetings in Newcastle, but the authorities put him out of the borough, conducting him to a "blew stane" on Tyne Bridge, that marked the extent of the Corporation jurisdiction. In 1658, he went again to the Eastern Counties, and made the acquaintance of the inside of Ipswich Gaol, being committed on a charge trumped up by one priest Willan. There he lay until Oliver Cromwell's death. About this time he maintained several public controversies: the most notable being one with Dr. Richard Smith, keeper of the University library at Cambridge. They argued in public, at meetings, both at Cambridge and at Westminster. Smith undertook to prove that Whitehead was a heretic. He put his proof into the form of syllogism:

He that is a Quaker is a heretic;
But you are Papists, (*i. e.*, the Quakers);
Ergo, you are a heretic.

Whitehead, who was well educated, and no mean logician, (indeed he would have made a good lawyer, to judge from the legal arguments advanced by him on various occasions on his own defence,) denied the minor premiss, which Dr. Smith tried to prove, by asserting that all who refused the oath of allegiance were Papists—therefore the Quakers were Papists. Whitehead afterwards refuted Smith in two books, one called "Truth defending the Quakers," and the other, "The Key of Knowledge not found in the University Library of Cambridge." Of Whitehead's other public controversies, some were conducted in churches, he arguing from a pew, and the parson from his pulpit. Whitehead, in addition to the qualities we have mentioned, of good education, knowledge of logic and of law, appears to have possessed a cool and imperturbable temper, and a readiness of repartee which gave him great advantage in wordy contests, whether waged with theological disputants in the pulpit, or with country justices on the bench.

The first part of Whitehead's journal, from which we have derived our information about him, was published under the name of his Christian Progress, and ends with an account of his being mobbed at Peterborough, and rescued by some soldiers of "Lambert's, or the Old Army." This was just before the Restoration. He also describes the agitation, which was stirred up among the "Proud and Covetous Priests, and Mercenary Teachers of all Sorts," by the report of a people risen in the north of England, called Quakers. The priests and the preachers were, he writes, afraid that their trade was in danger, and their gain at stake. "Then rung the Pulpits, and Lectures were promoted, and Conferences, Complaints, and Petitions exhibited to Magistrates, against the *Quakers*, under the unjust and false pretences of their being Antichrists, come in the Last Days; Deceivers, Seducers, dangerous to Church and State."

The second part of the "Christian Progress" begins with the Restoration. In our account of George Fox, we stated that Quakers then ceased for a brief space to be persecuted. This cessation lasted only for a few months; for so long the King adhered to his declaration of religious liberty, written at Breda; and then, in consequence of the plot of the Fifth-Monarchy-Men, a severe proclamation was issued against Anabaptists, Quakers, and Fifth-Monarchy-Men. Under this, great persecution raged. Whitehead was not long in being again committed to prison. On this occasion he was confined in the Vice, a hole, without a chimney, in the Castle-wall of Norwich. Here four of them spent the winter without a fire, except the luxury of a little charcoal, at the risk of suffocation. Whitehead was brought up before Judge Wadham Wyndham, at Thetford assizes, and indicted for refusing to take the oath of allegiance. Whitehead would not plead, and fruitlessly addressed the judge, who had, however, in the words, "'Take him away, gaoler,' an argument that could not be disputed." He was sent back to Norwich, but got his release in March, 1661, under a royal proclamation, after sixteen weeks' confinement. In that same year, a very severe Act was framed by the Legislature against Quakers; while it was in committee, George Whitehead, Richard Hubberthorne, and Edward Burrough, appeared against it before the Committee, and afterwards before the House, which they addressed from the bar with sound and practical arguments, which had no effect, for the bill passed: it prohibited all meetings of more than five Quakers, under heavy penalties. Under this Act, their meetings in London were broken up by the trained bands, and the three we have mentioned sent to Newgate, where Hubberthorne and Burrough sank and died under the hardships of their confinement. Newgate was then divided into two sides, Chapel side and Justice Hall side. On the latter side the richer prisoners were kept. The chief persecutor of

Friends in London was Alderman Sir Richard Brown. After being released from Newgate, Whitehead was again arrested at a meeting held at Horsleydown, and committed, after a skilful defence made by himself, by the Surrey justices, to White Lion Prison, in Southwark. So persecuted, indeed, was the Society at this time, that Whitehead writes that he always took his nightcap in his pocket when he went to a meeting, for fear he should be carried off from it to prison. To relate all the occasions on which he was sent to prison, is impossible. While in White Lion Prison, Whitehead, in 1663, was taken to Whitehall, and charged with being accessory to the dangerous plot of the Westmorland fanatics, under Captain Atkinson, of Mallerstang, known as the "Kipper Rigg Plot." He was examined, but the charge against him was dropped, and he heard no more of it.

Whitehead was in London during the plague, and also during the great fire, and gives, in the "Christian Progress," accounts of both. The Bull and Mouth, the Society's original place of meeting in London, was destroyed by the fire. They had also meeting places at the Peel, in St. John's Street, Westminster; at Horsleydown, in Southward; at Ratcliff; at Devonshire House, in Bishopsgate; and at a place called Old Buildings. After the fire they built a place in White Hart

Court, Gracechurch Street. The climax, perhaps, of the sufferings of the Society, was an Order in Council to Sir Christopher Wren, to pull down their meeting house at Horsleydown, which was done; and, when the Friends met on the spot where it had been, they were dispersed, in a very barbarous manner, by foot and horse soldiers.

After twelve years of persecution, lasting from 1660 to 1672, a Declaration of Indulgence to Dissenters was published. Under this, the Society had some rest; but an immense number, over four hundred, of its members were actually in prison. Whitehead, with two others, attended at the Council Chamber, and addressed the King on their behalf, and got a promise of a pardon from him. This pardon Whitehead carried through, though he had great difficulties with the law officers, and others, both over law points and over fees. It was, too, no easy matter to get so bulky a document as a pardon for four hundred people shown to all the sheriffs in England; but, by Whitehead's legal knowledge and ingenuity, all difficulties were surmounted.

The Declaration of Indulgence was withdrawn in 1674, and persecution again commenced; but the King, in 1679, on Whitehead's application, in some degree mitigated it. Whitehead and two other Friends, introduced by William Chiffins, had an interview on the subject with the King, in his closet. Whitehead believed that the King was really touched in conscience by his representations, and that his natural inclinations against persecution, and for liberty of conscience, were frustrated by those around him. In March, 1679, Whitehead, and a Friend named Burr, were sent to prison at Norwich. Over a hundred pages of the "Christian Progress" are taken up with an account of the legal, or rather illegal, proceedings against them; but we need hardly go into them. Whitehead argued his own case with unusual ability, displaying great knowledge of law and legal precedents; but he and Burr did not get their release until July, 1680.

About the time of their release, the Long Parliament had, by changes in its constitution, altered in disposition, and become mercifully inclined towards the Society of Friends. A Committee was appointed to consider their case; and Whitehead, William Penn, and others, were examined before it. Bills were brought in for their relief, but the dissolution stopped their progress. Sir Christopher Musgrave, of Edenhall, in Cumberland, the Tory leader, and a zealous Church of England man, used strong language over these bills, advocating, much to Whitehead's surprise, that toleration should be exhibited to Friends. Another bill, with the same object, miscarried in the next Parliament, being either designedly mislaid, or else stolen, when it should have been presented for the royal assent.

Whitehead at this time appears to have become the leader of the Society, and its official mouthpiece. We find him, on several occasions, going to the King, and asking for toleration and mercy on behalf of the Society, over a thousand of whose members were, *circa* 1684 or 1685, in various prisons. On one occasion, he addressed the King in Council, being, by royal permission, covered. On other occasions, the difficulty of the hats was easily got over: once, he had an audience with the King in Hampton Park, when an usher gently removed Whitehead's hat, and hung it upon the park palings. The King always received Whitehead with readiness, and occasionally discussed with him the practices of not uncovering the head, and of using Thee and Thou, which, the King maintained, was affectation. Up to the end of this reign, Whitehead continued to be fined for preaching, and the fines were taken by levies on his goods.

With the reign of James II., a new era commenced for the Society of Friends. Whitehead lost no time in making personal application to the new monarch, and found him ready to grant almost all he was asked. He issued his warrant for a release of all Friends in prison, so far as he could by law. He appointed a Commission to question and examine the common informers, in London and Middlesex, against the Society. Under it, the tables were effectually turned, and some of those gentry were punished for perjury. In the conversations the King had with Whitehead, he was, no doubt, fishing for the Society's votes at the elections; indeed, he almost said as much, for he advised what manner of men they should vote for. He also assured Whitehead that he himself had always been for liberty of conscience. The famous Declaration of Indulgence which James II. issued was as great a boon to the Friends as to the Papists, and after it we can gather little more from Whitehead's Journal. The "Christian Progress" jumps from the reign of James II. to that of William III., affording no clue as to what the Society thought of the change of Government. It, indeed, becomes very meagre in the information it gives; but Whitehead was growing in years, and the cessation of persecution made his days less eventful. We find Whitehead, after the Restoration, attending the House of Commons, and speaking before a Committee, or at the bar, in favour of measures advantageous to the Society. He also headed a deputation to William III., to discuss the payment of tithes and the taking of oaths, and so impressed the King, that, as Whitehead was afterwards told, he himself maintained the deputation's honesty in argument with some of his lords. During this reign, Whitehead, by strenuous exertions, procured the passing of an Act, by which Friends might affirm, instead of having to swear. To get this bill through, he himself saw and interviewed most of its opponents, and did his best to disarm their opposition. All his life, Whitehead continued to keep a close watch over all Parliamentary bills that might affect the Society, and by his exertions secured considerable alleviations for it. When Peter the Great was in England, Whitehead headed a deputation to him, with an address, but they did not obtain an interview. The "Christian Progress" closes in 1711, when Whitehead was about seventy-four.

In 1714, he attended with an address from the Society to King George I., on his accession to the throne, and, after the presentation of the address, made a congratulatory speech to him. He also had an interview with the Prince of Wales, by whom he was very kindly received. In 1715, after the suppression of the rebellion, and again in 1716, he presented congratulatory addresses to the King. Even in his eighty-sixth year, he employed his pen, and produced a small treatise, called "An Epistle to our Christian Friends."

George Whitehead died in 1722–3, aged eighty-seven, and was buried in that *Campus Sacer* of Dissent, Bunhill Fields. For long he kept a grocer's shop in London. He was twice married, first, in 1670, to a widow, Anne Downer, who died in 1686. In 1688, he married Ann Goddard, who kept a shop in Whitechapel, and was daughter of Captain Richard Goddard, a clothier, of Reading. Whitehead had no children.

MILES HALHEAD.

Miles Halhead was a husbandman at Mount-joy, near Underbarrow, and became, when of the age of thirty-eight, one of George Fox's earliest converts. He was the first Friend that was ever imprisoned in Kendal Gaol. Soon after his convincement, he felt impelled, by a vision, to go to Kendal Church, and call the priest "a painted hypocrite," — a performance for which Justice Archer committed Halhead to prison, where his detention was not very long. He was, too, one of the earliest preachers of the Society that went into the South of England. In Sewell's History of the Friends, and in an account of his imprisonments, published in 1690, we find many accounts of sufferings which Halhead underwent. At Swarthmore, in Yorkshire, the wife of Justice Preston, of Holkar Hall, set her servants to beat the unfortunate preacher, because he passed her without bowing. Halhead, indignant at this treatment, called her Jezebel, whereon the great lady spat in his face. Three months later, Halhead called at Holkar Hall, and asked to see Thomas

Preston's wife. It so happened that she herself came to the door; but, from shame, or what not, she denied herself, and tried to palm off another woman as Mrs. Preston. Miles, having such good reason to recollect her, was not to be deceived, and read her a lesson on lying, which must have been felt. She did not again set her servants on him. This was in 1653. In the same year, Halhead visited Skipton, Bradford, Leeds, Halifax, Doncaster, and York, at all of which places he preached, meeting with great opposition. At Skipton he was so beaten by the mob, that he was left for dead, but recovered, miraculously, in the space of three hours. At Doncaster, a similar beating happened to him, and he was put to bed by his friends. However, he struggled out, got to a chapel, and began to preach. Ere he finished, all his bruises were again "miraculously" healed. At York, he had the Lord Mayor among his audience.

Shortly after his return home from this journey, he lost a child, a boy of about five, to whom his wife was much attached. This was the occasion of her conversion; previously, she had been much discontented with her husband's absence on preaching tours, and was wont to lament that she had not rather married a drunkard: "Then I might have found him at the alehouse: but now I cannot tell where to find my husband." Prior to the child's death, she had a vision, in which she heard a voice warning her not to be discontented with her husband's journeys, or else a greater cross would fall upon her. This threatened cross she recognised when her child died. In other journeys, Halhead underwent much suffering. At Stanley Chapel, in Lancashire, Captain William Rawlinson and another man took him by the head and feet, and pitched him over the wall of the chapel yard. He suffered from this much, but resolutely went on to Windermere Church, where he preached to the priest and the people, and his "bruises were healed that day." He next visited Furness, and entered the church, where the priests, Lampitt and Camelford, declined to go on with the service until he was removed. We, shortly after this, hear of him at Newcastle, where the Mayor and Sheriff committed him to prison, but very soon let him go, the Mayor being troubled with doubts as to whether they had done right in imprisoning him.

In 1654, Halhead visited Ireland, in company with James Lancaster and Miles Bateman, and then proceeded to Scotland, crossing probably by Portpatrick, for Dumfries was the first Scottish town he came to. Here, Halhead commenced to preach one Sunday, in the Kirk of Dumfries, but was turned out, and only escaped stoning at the hands of the women of the town by pulling off his clothes, and wading through the Nith. He journeyed thence, by Edinburgh, Leith, Glasgow, and Stirling, to Berwick-on-Tweed, where he was lodged in the gaol for ten weeks,—a confinement which his zeal brought on his head. The first thing he did, on entering the town, was to go to the Mayor's shop, and call his worship a persecutor, who, not unnaturally, sent Halhead to prison. There he remained until the sessions, when he was brought before the Mayor and the justices. The Mayor was anxious to let Halhead go, wished he had never seen him, and hoped to be no more troubled with him. Halhead, however, made a speech, in which he repeated his offence, and appealed to the Recorder to say that his committal was illegal, on the ground that the Mayor had acted as both judge and prosecutor. This the Recorder was obliged to admit. The Court ordered the gaoler to take Halhead away, and shortly afterwards granted his release. From Berwick, Halhead went to York and Hull, and thence, by Lincolnshire, Leicestershire, London, and Exeter, to Plymouth, where he was imprisoned many months, on a charge of having called a drunken naval chaplain a thief. General Desborough interfered on behalf of the prisoners,—for one Salthouse was confined on the same charge; but they were, spite of his intercession, not released in a hurry. We have little further record of Halhead's travels. In 1666, he again visited

Devonshire, and was taken before the magistrates, who asked him his business there. Halhead replied, with great coolness, that he came to see his friends, and named Sir John Copplestone, the Sheriff of Devonshire, John Page, the Mayor of Plymouth, Justice Howel, and Colonel Buffet, the authorities who had committed him to prison on his last visit. He learnt that all these men were in poverty and disgrace, having been turned out of their estates and offices at the Restoration.

In 1673, we find Halhead again at Plymouth. On this occasion, he got permission to see General Lambert, then condemned to perpetual imprisonment on an island in the harbour. In the course of a very interesting interview, Halhead told Lambert, in plain language, that his downfall, and that of Cromwell, was due to their having permitted the Society of Friends to be persecuted. This lecture Lambert took in good part, and, when it was over, called for beer, and drank with Halhead, and they afterwards talked over the battle of Dunbar, on whose field Halhead had been the week after the fight, and the various officers of the Commonwealth before whom Halhead had, on several occasions, been examined, namely, Generals Fleetwood and Desborough, Major Blackmore, and Colonel Fenwick. In the following year, 1674, Halhead wrote a letter to George Fox, and describes himself as old, infirm, and weak of sight; and that is the last information we have of him.

In the year 1664, when Halhead would be about fifty years old, he was summoned to Kendal, before the Chancellor of the Bishop of Chester, for non-attendance at public worship. Being asked by the Chancellor to give a plain reason for his conduct, Halhead replied, that he had heard the priests preach for thirty years, and had observed that they, in one year, always contradicted what they had said the year before. The Chancellor excommunicated Halhead,—a penalty for which he, probably, cared but little.

JOHN BURNYEAT.

JOHN BURNYEAT was born at Crabtreebeck, in the parish of Loweswater, in Cumberland, about 1630. He was one of those who were convinced by George Fox, in 1653. As he puts it himself, he saw that his profession of religion was but as "Adam's Fig-leaf Apron, in which he could not abide God's coming." Burnyeat, and some others, established meetings twice a week; but, until 1657, he was not concerned to travel much, except to visit Friends that were in prison for religion's sake. Burnyeat soon found himself in Carlisle Gaol. First of all, he visited the "Bell-house" at Aspetry (Aspatria), and, after being hurried away once by the people, and retiring to Plumbland Common for meditation, he returned in the afternoon, and had a controversy with Priest Warwick, in the graveyard, and did not spare him. At Lorton and Loweswater, he went to the "Worship-house," and was threatened, by Priest Fogoe, with the stocks. At Brigham, he went to the church, and commenced to preach when Priest Denton had done. The people beat Burnyeat with their Bibles and with sticks. He was arrested by the constable, and taken before Lancelot Fletcher, of Tallantyre, who committed him to Carlisle Gaol, where he remained three-and-twenty weeks before he was released. In 1658, he commenced his travels. His journal has been published, but is little more than an itinerary. His travels extended through Ireland, Scotland, Barbadoes, Virginia, Maryland, New Jersey, Long and Rhode Islands, and New England. He was the companion of George Fox in America, who writes of him: "He travelled with me from Maryland, through the wilderness, and through many rivers and desperate bogs, where, they said, never Englishman nor horse had travelled before: where we lay out at nights, and sometimes in Indian houses, and many times were very hard put to it for provisions.

Burnyeat died at Dublin, in 1690. His journal, and some tracts and letters, were published in 1691.

JOHN WILKINSON AND JOHN STORY.

We have, in an account of George Fox, mentioned one JOHN WILKINSON, as having three churches, or "steeple-houses," near Cockermouth, one of which was Brigham; and we have also mentioned that Fox preached in two of his churches. William Penn, in his Preface to the Life of John Banks, mentions "Cumberland John Wilkinson," as "formerly an able and zealous Independent preacher." It is probable that the original incumbents of Wilkinson's churches were turned out of their posts during the Commonwealth, and that Wilkinson, Independent though he was, acquired them in some way or other. The hold which Fox's teaching took upon the common people in Cumberland gradually deprived Wilkinson of his congregation, and he at last established a meeting of the few that remained to him, and preached to them at his own house. He next set up "a silent meeting, like the Friends;" but one by one the attendants thereat dwindled down to half-a-dozen or so, while most of the deserters joined the Society of Friends. Thus left alone,

Wilkinson began to come to the meetings of Friends on Pardshaw Crag, where several hundreds were wont to assemble. "Here he would prowl around the outskirts," says Fox, "like a shepherd looking for his sheep." In 1657, Fox attended one of these meetings, and to this Wilkinson came, with all his remaining flock, now reduced to about four. After the meeting, Wilkinson had some talk with Fox, was convinced, gave up his livings and became a minister in the Society. His name, as "Cumberland John Wilkinson," occurs several times in the journals of John Banks and Christopher Story.

This is not that Wilkinson who associated himself with one JOHN STORY, a Westmorland Friend, of whom we know little, except that he was once in Salisbury Gaol, and that he died in Wilkinson's lifetime, aged about forty-five. These two became discontented with the management of the Society's business, stirred up divisions against George Fox, and formed, under the name of Separatists, a new branch of the Society. They were joined by other preachers, of the names of Rogers, Crisp, Harris, and Keith, of whom the latter attained considerable celebrity. The Separatists objected, among other things, to the laying down of rules for the government of the Society's affairs, and they objected strongly to women's meetings. Their practices, too, were looser than those of the original

Society; and thus they gained followers among many who feared to go the lengths ventured by the original Society. The Separatists, for instance, used to pay tithes under protest, instead of resisting to the last. Under Keith, this new branch grew to be an important schism in the Society, and is frequently mentioned by Story, of Justus Town, in his journal. It took place about 1683, and its first head-quarters were in Westmorland.

Cumberland John Wilkinson died in 1675, "after he had continued many years," writes Fox, in his journal, "in the free ministry of Jesus."

THOMAS LAWSON.

THOMAS LAWSON was the son of Sir Thomas and Ruth, Lady Lawson, and was not only an eminent minister of the Church of England, but was also a scholar of great attainments, and a "herbalist," or botanist, second to none of his day in England. He held a cure at a small place called Ramside. Hearing, by chance, that George Fox was coming to Ramside one Sunday, Lawson not only recommended his congregation to go and hear him, and for that purpose suspended his own afternoon sermon, but actually placed his chapel and pulpit at Fox's disposal, and took up a place among the audience. Lawson was himself convinced, and resigned his cure of souls, as a proof of his sincerity: he became a "ministering Friend," but does not appear to have travelled much, or far. He settled at Great Strickland, in Westmorland, and opened there a school, which became both large and famous. There he spent the rest of his life. Dying, in 1691, at the age of fifty-five, he was buried at Newby Head, and some of his pupils erected a monument to him, with the following inscription:—

> "Sub hoc Tumulo, jacet Corpus Thomæ Lawson, de Magnæ Stricklandiæ. Ludi Magister, et Botanicus non imperitus, qui obiit 12 Die Novembri, Anno Domini 1691, Anno Ætatis 55."

His wife, and only son, a lad of great piety, sleep with him in the same tomb.

JOHN BANKS.

John Banks, of Brigham, was a celebrated preacher among the Society of Friends, and the hero, while in prison in Carlisle, of an adventure with the Mayor of that city. This John Banks was a Cumberland man, and is generally known as John Banks, of Brigham. A memoir of him was published in 1712, under the title of "A Journal of the Life, Labours, Travels, and Sufferings, in and for the Gospel, of that ancient Servant and faithful Minister of Jesus Christ, John Banks." To it is added a collection of his letters and papers, and the Preface is written by William Penn himself. There have been several subsequent editions of this Memoir, all more or less abridged: the first and unmutilated edition is now rarely to be met with.

John Banks, as he tells us in this journal, "came of honest parents:" he was the only child of William and Emme *(sic in origine)* Banks, and was born in 1638, at Sunderland, in the parish of Isel, or Issell (as he writes it), in Cumberland. His father was a fellmonger and glover, but also took land to farm. A few years after John's birth, his people moved to "within the compass of Pardshow-meeting." Pardshaw, to use the modern name, is a hamlet, about four miles from Cockermouth, in the parish of Dean; and the Banks family settled at Brigham, which is the adjoining parish to that of Dean. The doctrines of the Society of Friends spread at a very early date in this neighbourhood; and their founder, George Fox, in his journal mentions attending general meetings of the Society at Pardshaw Crag. In 1645, John Banks was sent to school, and remained there for seven years, until he was fourteen; he learned well both English and Latin, and could write well,—accomplishments which he forthwith utilised, by teaching school at Dissington, or Distington. Here he remained a year, and then moved to Mosser Chappel, near Pardshaw, where he taught school, and "read the Scriptures also, to People that came there on the First Day of the Week, and Homily, as it is called, and Sung Psalms, and Prayed: But I have no liking to the Practice: But my Father, with other People, through my entering into Reasoning with them, overcame me." Here Banks had twenty-four scholars, for each of whom he received twelvepence a quarter; he also received, for his religious services, twelvepence a year from every house of them that came to hear him, a fleece of wool, and his table free. Mosser Chappel, where he officiated, was merely a chapel of ease to the "Parish Steeple House," which was some miles off. One day, when Banks was officiating, there came to hear him, among the rest of the people that were indifferent where they did go for worship, one John Fletcher, "a great scholar, but a Drunken, Sottish Man." Fletcher, after service one day, called Banks aside, and told him, he read very well for a youth, but he did not "pray in form, as others used to do," and promised to send him a letter of instructions. When this letter arrived, it contained a form of prayer for Banks to use. As he was considering it, the words of St. Paul came to his mind, in which the Apostle declared, that he had the Gospel he had to preach, not from man, but by the revelation of Jesus Christ. Being thus aroused, the result of Banks's thoughts was a visit to "the meeting of the People in Scorn called Quakers." From this time, Banks became a member of the Society of Friends. He states, in his journal, that he was sixteen years and four months when it pleased the Lord to touch his heart,—an event which he dates as happening in the Tenth Month, 1654. He gave up his scholastic duties; indeed, after the receipt of Fletcher's letter, he never again officiated at the chapel, and declined to receive the wages due to him. He learnt his father's trades, both as a fellmonger and glover, and also as a farmer; and had shortly the happiness of seeing both his parents become Friends. It was, however, nearly six years before the doubts stirred up by Fletcher's epistle quite subsided, and Banks became settled in his mind. In 1659, Banks was at a meeting of Friends, on Pardshaw Crag, when he was moved to go to the steeple-house at Cockermouth, which he did, but was turned out at once, by order of "the hireling priest, George Larcum," or Larkham, mentioned in our account of George Fox, for coming in with his hat on his head. Banks, however, returned, and followed Larcum's sermon with one of his own, which made "the Hireling Fly, with all the haste he could, out at a contrary Door than he used to do." Another result was, to create a great tumult, in the midst of which Banks was again haled out of the church, after which, he writes, "I came away in sweet Peace and spiritual Comfort in my Heart and Soul."

An hiatus of three or four years now occurs in the journal. In 1663, we find Banks at a meeting of Friends upon the Howhill, near Caldbeck, in Cumberland, "whereunto came George Fletcher, of Hutton Hall, a Justice of the Peace, so called, who came into the Meeting Rude and Unmannerly, Riding among Friends, they sitting upon the Ground, and Trode with his Horse feet upon a Woman's Gown that was Big with Child, a Woman of Note, and Well-bred; and I was moved of the

Lord to kneel down in Prayer at the Head of his Horse." Sir George struck Banks with a horsewhip over his head and face, and then ordered his servant to take Banks away. He was, accordingly, dragged away, by the hair of his head, down the hill on which the meeting was held. Banks, on recovering his feet, asked Sir George the very pertinent question, "Dost thou pretend to be a Justice of Peace, and breaks the Peace, and Disturbs, Persecutes, and Abuses God's peaceable People, and sets on thy Servant so to do?" Sir George proved his right to the title of Justice of the Peace, for he fined Banks five pounds, and in default committed him to Carlisle Gaol, where, says Banks, "George Martin, a wicked, hard-hearted Man, being Gaoler, put us in the Common Gaol, several Days and Nights, without either Bread or Water; because we could not answer nor satisfie his Covetous desire in giving him eightpence a Meal for our Meat; so he threatened, when he put us in the Common Gaol, he would see how long we could live there without Meat, and did suffer none that he could hinder, neither would he suffer any of our friends to bring us any Bedding, not so much as a little Straw, so that we had no place to Lie on, but the Prison Window, upon the Cold Stones; the Wall being thick, there was Room for one at a time. And when he saw he could not Prevail, notwithstanding his Cruelty, he moved us from the Common Gaol into a Room in his own House, where he had several Friends Prisoners for Non-Payment of Tythes at the suit of the said George Fletcher." Quarter Sessions came round in about a fortnight after Banks had been imprisoned; he and his companions were called before that gallant cavalier, Sir Philip Musgrave, whom Banks writes of as "called a Justice, but an old Persecutor." Musgrave asked the imprisoned Friends to conform to the Established Church, and promised, in that event, to favour them as far as he could. He, however, would listen to nothing from them but a direct answer to his questions, telling them not to preach there, and adding, "When you are banished to beyond the seas," (the penalty for the third offence against the Act under which Banks had been committed,) "then you may preach there." In the end, Musgrave and the magistrates ordered the release of the prisoners, and that their goods should be taken in payment of the fines. Banks complains that a cow and horse of his father's, worth £6 10s., were distrained in payment of the fine of £5, for which Fletcher committed him. What followed before the prisoners were released, is worthy to be told in the words of Banks himself. It is a funny picture of prison discipline:—

"So we were set at Liberty that Sessions, Goods being taken for all our Fines. Only the Sheriff for the County,

Willfred Lawson, of Issel Hall, being there, said to the Gaoler, If they will not Pay Fees, put them into the Common Gaol again, and keep them there until they Rot. So the Gaoler did put us in the Common Gaol again, because we could not Pay him Fees; where was a Bedlam Man, and four with him for Theft; and two notorious Thieves, called Redhead and Wadelad; two Mosstroopers, for stealing of Cattle; and one Woman for Murthering of her own Child. Now, several of the Relations and Acquaintances of these were suffered to come to see them, after the Sessions was over, who gave them so much Drink that they were basely Drunk, most of them; and, the Prison being a close, nasty Place, they did so Abuse themselves and us, with doing all their Necessaries so undecently, that it was enough almost to stifle some of us: So on the Morrow we let the Gaoler know how we were Abused. Whereupon he bid the Turnkey bring us to the room where we were before; he scorned to keep us there; we were Honest Men, setting our Religion aside. One of us answered, If the Tree be Good, the Fruit cannot be Evil. So, in a little time after we had been in his house, he gave us our Liberty, without Paying of Fees. This was in the Fifth Month, 1663."

Certainly, this account presents a strange picture of Carlisle Gaol in 1663. From a letter, written by Banks, we find that he had four companions in this imprisonment, and one of them was Mungo Bewley, an inhabitant of Carlisle. The common gaol was in the old Citadel of Carlisle.

In the following year, Banks married his first wife, Ann Littledale. By her he appears to have had six children,—John, William, Sarah, Mary, Ann, and Emma. Four years after he commenced wedded life, he felt himself called to travel, in the work of the ministry, towards the South and West of England. His companion was Cumberland John Wilkinson. This journey lasted two months, and was in length twelve hundred and sixty-eight miles,—no little distance, when roads were almost unknown, and packhorses had not been superseded by wheeled conveyances. Banks, in his journal, enters into no detail as to his journeys, and, indeed, intimates an intention of only recording what may be material. He states, with laudable pride, that he had gone over-sea, betwixt England, Scotland, and Ireland, twelve times, "and that often not without great Difficulty and Danger of Life at Sea, by many Tempestuous Storms; yet never, at any time, was I above two Nights together at Sea: insomuch that, after sometimes that I had taken Shipping at White-Haven, the Sea-Men would be very desirous who should have me in their Vessel; saying, 'I was the Happiest Man that ever they Carried over Sea, for they got well along still when they had me.'" Banks inserts in his journal his letters, written while travelling, to his wife and children, and to his apprentice, Peter Fearon, afterwards a preacher, and companion of his master; and, also, letters from his wife to him. She dates from "Whinfell Hall, in Cumberland." One or two of the few adventures which he relates are worth mention. At Wicklow, in Ireland, a place to which he was directed to go, in a dream, he was arrested by a sergeant and a guard of musketeers, and brought before Governor Hamman, his man, the priest, and his wife. Banks was committed to the county gaol, at the instigation of the priest's wife, who was by far the most zealous of his opponents. The gaoler, however, allowed Banks to hold a large meeting in prison; and, when the Sheriff remonstrated, the gaoler asserted his right to let his prisoners do what they pleased, come and go as they liked, provided they were in prison when wanted. The party was not detained long; for the Governor, when the priest and priest's wife were not at hand to earwig him, gave orders to release Banks and his two companions. The gaoler at first demanded fees before he would let them go, but, on discussion, waived his right. Banks thereon called for drink, (the gaoler was a publican,) and each of the party gave him twelvepence, with which he seemed much pleased. This visit to Wicklow resulted in the establishment of a large colony of Friends in that place.

In 1677, Banks lost, by paralysis apparently, the use of his arm and shoulder. He dreamt, one night, that he was with George Fox, the founder of the Society of Friends, and that he addressed him thus: "George, my Faith is such, that if thou seest it thy way to lay thy Hand upon my Shoulder, my Arm and Hand shall be whole throughout." This dream made such an impression upon Banks, that he went to Yorkshire in search of Fox, related the dream, and he records that, on Fox laying his hand on the afflicted shoulder, it began to, and actually did, heal. "And the next time," writes Banks, "that G. F. and I met, he readily said, *John, thou mended, thou mended;* I answer'd, Yes, very well, in a little time."

Banks continued to travel, as a preacher, through England, Scotland, and Ireland, until 1684, in which year he was again sent to prison at Carlisle, by Sir George Fletcher, who was the lay impropriator of tithes, which Banks refused to pay. Banks heads the portion of his journal, in which he relates his imprisonment, thus:—

"Here followeth a Relation of my Imprisonment in the City of Carlisle, in Cumberland; which was Six Years and Nine Months, because for Conscience' sake I could not Pay Tythes demanded by George Fletcher, of Hutton Hall, in the asad. County, a Justice of the Peace so called, but a great Persecutor of God's People, by Imprisonment, and spoiling their Goods, and if he had had all of me, at the time of my Commitment, that he pretended was his Due, it was but Eight Shillings and Sixpence; which sheweth his Hard-heartedness and Oppression."

George Martin, the former keeper of Carlisle Gaol, had been succeeded in that office by George Lancake, who had, for his turnkey, Alexander Richardson. At first, Lancake kept Banks, and twelve other Friends, all of whom had refused to pay tithes, in his house, which was in Castle Street, near the great steeple-house, as the Friends called the Cathedral. Of this proximity Banks availed himself, to address the people attending worship there from the gaoler's window,—a practice which was highly disapproved of by the authorities. Our hero writes to his wife: "The Mayor, Aldermen, and Priests here fright the gaoler with Threatenings about my Speaking out at the Casement; and he threatens what he will do to me, if I will not be silent." Lancake carried out his threats, and thrust Banks into a noisome, smoky room over a brewhouse, and kept him there without a bed. When he sent for Banks to come forth, the prisoner declined to do so, until Lancake himself should come and fetch him,—a defiance to which Lancake's reply was, that Banks might stay where he was till he rotted before he would fetch him. The result, however, was, that Banks got the victory, though not until the turnkey had tried to drag him out by main force, and failed. Lancake had then himself to eat humble pie, and conduct his prisoner out of the room over the brewhouse, which he did with the words, "Pray God I had never seen thy face." His chagrin at his defeat was by no means lessened by the fact, that the debtors in his custody had foretold it, and had the pleasure of witnessing the fulfilment of their prophecy. Under the prison regulations of the time, the prisoners were allowed to go out into the town. Banks complains greatly that the turnkey was sent after him to Friends' meetings, and dragged him out, back to the gaoler's house, whenever he began to speak. At last, Lancake put a stop to this laxity of imprisonment, and confined his Quaker prisoners to the court-yard of his house, and refused them leave to go out, even to buy provisions. This rigour did not prevent meetings of Friends being held in the gaoler's house, at which people of the town were present. John Carlisle is mentioned, as expounding at one of these, and as being turned out by the gaoler, or the turnkey, who had adopted the plan of knocking Banks's hat over his eyes whenever he began to exhort, and of hooting to drown his voice, while, at times, they locked him up in the smoky room over the brewhouse. At last occurred the scene we have alluded to above. We transcribe the account of it given by Banks; it is mentioned by other writers:—

"Now, about this time, upon the First Day of the Week, the then Mayor, John How, and Aldermen, with the Chief-Priests, there being a great Rabble of them belonging to the City, with several of a Persecuting Spirit, being greatly enraged against me, because I was often constrained, by the Power of God, to sound Truth's Testimony in their ears, as they came from their Worship, I being in their view, the Casement of our Window being open to the Street. Upon the aforesaid Day, the Mayor and Aldermen, with others, came into our Meeting in our Prison-house, when I was in my Testimony of Truth; and the Mayor, in great Fury and Rage, bid me be silent, often shaking his Staff at me, threatening what he would do to me for Preaching there, and disturbing all the City, in Contempt of Authority. I seemed to take no notice of him for some time, that so he might manifest himself the more; he, being a very Passionate Man, said, if I would not be Silent, he would Stop my Mouth. Then I answered and said, the Lord had opened my Mouth, and he, and all the Assistance he could get in the City, could not stop it. But he said he would put a Gagg in it, and put me in the Common Gaol, and I should Preach there to the Walls. I said, I neither fear thee, thy Gagg, nor the Common Gaol; for though thou art the Mayor, thou hast nothing to do to meddle with us; we are the King's Prisoners, and in safe Custody, and here is our Keeper, (pointing at the Gaoler, he being present,) so thou mayest go about thy own Business; with which, he was silent. Then one of the Aldermen said to me, he could prove I had nothing to do to Preach. I asked him, how he could prove it? He said, by the Bible. I bid one reach him a Bible quickly. Another Alderman said to him, Let him alone, Sir, you will do no good with him, you may as well speak to the Wall. So he failed of his proof, and with some Threatening Words they all went, to their Shame and Discredit, and troubled us no more."

Lancake next tried to cajole and flatter Banks into holding his tongue, representing that the Mayor would fine him (Lancake) for permitting an illegal conventicle to be held in his house. This representation had no effect, and Banks was at last removed into the common gaol, where were the poor debtors and the thieves. Here he suffered great hardship, and was treated with great ignominy, which was extended to his wife, who, when she visited her husband, was made to spend the night with him in the common gaol. From the gaol, Banks addressed a paper to the inhabitants of Carlisle, complaining of his treatment, and exhorting them to repent of their sins. He mentions that he had often seen, with pain, both men and women cursing, and swearing, and reeling drunk in Carlisle streets. Perhaps in consequence of this paper, perhaps because Lancake concluded, as he told the aldermen, that nought but sewing up his mouth could stop Banks from preaching, the rigour of his captivity was, from this time, much mitigated. Lancake hired another house, with a court-yard enclosed with gates, and with rooms at the back. Here, Banks could expound freely, unheard in the streets. He was again allowed to go about Carlisle, and even to go home occasionally. When in confinement, Banks worked at his trade, as a fellmonger and glover, in prison; but much sitting, and the cold he endured in one very severe winter, when sixteen were confined in one room, with "but one little fire," "surfeited his body, and he grew infirm." Many of his companions obtained their liberty, under King James's Proclamation of Indulgence, which, as Macaulay observes, and we have noticed before, favoured alike the two extremes, the Catholics and the Quakers. Banks himself, being imprisoned for tithes, did not benefit thereby, but was released under a proclamation of William III. He immediately resumed his travels, and took with him Thomas Story, (Thomas of Justus Town,) who, at this date, writes of Banks, as "that good, old, and valiant Soldier and Warrior for Truth on Earth,—John Banks." In 1691, Banks lost his wife. On her deathbed, she had a vision that her eldest daughter, who lived two hundred miles away, was confined of a son. She sent her son, John, to the Post-office, and he found a letter there with the news. A few years after this, Banks settled in Somersetshire, where he married Hannah Champion, a widow. Up to 1704, he continued to travel as a minister; but gout at last compelled him to desist; and he died at Street, in Somerset, in 1710, of that complaint in his hands, aged seventy-three.

Banks's journal, and several of his epistles and papers, were published in 1712, with a Preface by William Penn, who mentions that he had known Banks for forty-four years, as "a heavenly minister of experimental religion, of a sound judgment, and pious practice, valiant for truth upon the earth, and ready to serve all in the love and peace of the Gospel." Testimonials to his merits are also borne by his wife, his children, by various meetings of Friends, and by John Boustead, of Aglionby, and Christopher Story, of Righead, celebrated preachers, whose careers we shall sketch presently. As an example of his writings, we extract the following, from a letter to one of his children. It is dated from his prison-house, in Carlisle:—

"And now unto you, Ann, and Mary, my daughters, and dear Children, whom I dearly Love, with all the rest, be sure you speak no ill one of the other, nor do none, no, not to any body; carry no Tales from one House to another; and when you are sent on an Errand, go and come quickly; and be Loving, Kind, and Respective one to the other, and to your Brethren, Sisters, and Servants, and help one another willingly in all things, but especially your dear Mother: be Dutiful and Obedient unto her in all things, I Charge you, (what she bids you do,) do it readily, and willingly, without murmuring. My dear Children, keep these my words in mind daily, concerning your dear Mother, and one another; and that you may all serve one another in Love.

"And now unto you, little William, and Emme, the youngest. My dear Children, be sure you Love one another; do not fall out by the way when you go to School, or coming Home; shout not, laugh not, do no hurt to any Lad nor Lass, and mind your Books well, that you may be good Schollars. Be sure you remembar what I say unto you, and, above all things, be Careful to do what your Mother bids you, and Love your Brother and Sisters. Dear Children, all of you mind your Books, Read the Holy Scriptures; and so the Lord Bless, Prosper, Keep, and Preserve you all together in Love, Unity, Peace, and Quietness; Fearing, Serving, and Loving of God with all your Hearts, and so one another, and then all will be well.

"I find a great alteration in my body, because of the Cruelty and Hard Usage of the Gaoler and his Turn-Key; together with the want of fresh Air; for I have had no Liberty to walk Abroad these several Months, and the Gaoler doth not suffer me to Speak or Pray in any one Meeting, after he hears me; for which the Lord will assuredly meet with him by his judgements."

Of the doctrine of retribution alluded to in the last paragraph of this letter, Banks was evidently a firm believer. He notes instances in his journal, and the reader's attention is directed thereto by a small hand in the margin, thus: George Martin, Banks's first gaoler at Carlisle, died a prisoner for debt in his own gaol; George Larcum, the hireling priest who turned Banks out of his church at Cockermouth, lost his living on the Restoration; and an informer, who, at Dulverton, in Somerset, drew on Banks and his friends the penalties imposed for holding an illegal conventicle, was hanged for murdering his wife.

Banks's public epistles and letters are mostly addresses to be read at meetings of Friends, which he could not attend, or letters to different bodies of Friends. They contain little suitable for quotation, though the tone of sincerity which pervades them, and the vigorous Saxon in which they are written, make them interesting readings. We will venture on a very brief extract or two. In the first we select, Banks is inveighing against the fashions of the world.

"But, alas! what shall I say; for, notwithstanding what I have already said, I am not yet clear; for there remains a Testimony with me, to be given against the Untruth-like Fashions that are too much practised (among men, as well as women,) who profess the Truth in a higher degree than others, who should be Patterns and Examples unto others: and that is, your too fashionable Coats, with superfluous Buttons, and many folds by the 'sides; with your

EXTRAVAGANT WIGGS, Curled and Powder'd, (like Men of the Times,) not fit to be put upon the Head of any Man professing Truth; though some are more extream than others; (and it is the Extream the Testimony of Truth is against,) and wearing Hats with three Corners, like the Prophane World; and taking example one of another, which shows the ill effects of Bad Examples. What, think you, will the next Generation be? Oh! Blush, and be ashamed of these things!"

Wigs were worn by many leaders among the early Friends; among others, by James Logan, Penn's secretary, and Chief-Justice of Pennsylvania. Penn, in 1685, issued a license to Lloyd, his Deputy-Governor in Pennsylvania, to wear a wig.

In another passage, Banks writes thus:—

"We were to bear our Testimony against that Confused Language of *Ye* and *You* to a single Person; (neither could we put off our Hats to any;) but were to use the plain and Truth-like Language of *Thee* and *Thou* to every Single Person, which too many now make a Light matter of, and do suffer their Children to *Ye* and *You* their parents, (as well as others,) who have professed the Truth long; so that our Ancient Testimony, and Truth-like Language, is too much lost by such."

Banks's daughter, Ann, married Stephen Scotten, Coventry, in 1700. In 1711, she felt a call to the ministry, and travelled to meetings in England for twenty-eight years. She died in 1739.

CHRISTOPHER AND BRIDGET STORY.

CHRISTOPHER STORY was born in April, 1648, at Righead, in the parish of Kirklinton, about six miles from Carlisle, and as much from Scotland. His father was Thomas Story, a younger brother of the family, of that name, that lived at Lake, in the same parish. We can trace no relationship between this family and the Storys of Justus Town; and, from the language in which Christopher alludes to George Story, brother of Thomas, of Justus Town, and whilom Rector of Kirklinton, it is evident none such existed. Christopher's mother was Elizabeth Parret, the eldest daughter of Christopher Parret, who had been Rector of Kirklinton from 1611 to 1643, and who had saved a little money, and purchased, and much improved, the estate at Righead, which Christopher Story afterwards inherited, and where his father and mother kept an inn. Thomas Story, the father, had been servant of Philip Musgrave, whom Christopher describes as "of *Ednil Hall*, Knight, (of an Ancient Family in the *County* of *Cumberland*,) who, in the time of the *Civil War* between the *King* and *Parliament*, was for the

King, underwent many *jeopardies,* to the Hazard of his Life; but when King *Charles* the *Second* was restored to the *Crown,* the said *Philip Musgrave* being in favour with him, had great Places of Profit and Trust under the *Government;* and then he rewarded my Father for his former service."

Christopher Story was an only son, and his parents commenced his education at a very early age. He excelled both in learning and steadiness, and so gained many friends. He frequently visited Ednil, or Eden Hall, in company with his father, and generally spent a portion of each year there, to learn breeding and good manners, and as a companion to Sir Philip's son, Thomas, afterwards fellow of Queen's College, Oxford, Prebendary of Durham, and Archdeacon and Dean of Carlisle. Thomas Musgrave was about the same age as Christopher Story; and it was Sir Philip's wish that young Story should accompany Thomas Musgrave to Oxford; of this Sir Philip was willing to bear the charge, if old Story would provide his son with the due preparatory education. This was agreed to, and Christopher Story remained at school until he was old enough, probably fourteen or fifteen, to go to Oxford. He did not, however, go; for his mother then interposed, saying, "that if he was educated at the college, it was much if he ever came to live in the country; and it might happen that he would sell the land, and live elsewhere; and, considering he was like to have sufficient to live upon, she would not consent that he should go." Christopher, accordingly, stayed at home, and devoted himself to the usual amusements of the young men of his day,—shooting with guns and bows, and card-playing, at which last he was very successful. He, however, writes, that he was preserved from many sins: though he was brought up in an inn, to which people of all sorts resorted, yet he was preserved from the sin of drunkenness; and he never loved the excessive smoking of tobacco. Of the place of his abode, he tells us that it "was in the *Border of England* when *Wickedness* of the grossest sort had swelled to that height, that Theft, *Robbery*, and *Bloodshed*, with many other crying sins, were so very frequent amongst People, that Hell (in that sense) had opened her mouth." Among the more respectable classes, the constant practice was to play cards on Sunday evening. From this, Story abstained, considering thereby that he might safely play at any other time. During this gay portion of his life, he was troubled with religious doubts, which he calmed by saying to himself, that it would be time enough to be religious when he got married,—an event which happened when he was eighteen. His father and mother selected for him a young woman whose parents were of good repute in the country, and that is all we know about her, except that her name was Bridget, and that she afterwards became a ministering Friend, and preached at meetings of Friends, not only in the counties adjacent to Cumberland, but also in Scotland and Ireland. Shortly after his marriage, a great fever went through the country, and Bridget Story took it. Christopher consulted a blind spaewife, who assured him that he would not take it; but he did; and this illness, and the consequent fear of death, affected the tone of his whole life. On his recovery, he attended diligently at church, but found something wanting in what he heard there: although the priests could tell him what sin was, and its reward, yet they could not tell him how to come out of sin. Hearing of a religious meeting at Longtown, he went there, and heard Cumberland John Wilkinson, who had formerly been an Independent preacher, but who was at that time a Friend. At another meeting of Friends, near Longtown, he heard the celebrated Robert Barclay, of Ury, author of the "Apology for the Doctrines held by Friends," who was travelling northwards. With him, Story wished to discuss some religious points; but Barclay was afraid of a disturbance, took his horse, and would not stay. Some other Friends took up Story's challenge, and, though he was aided by a young priest, yet he got the worst, and resolved never again publicly to dispute with Friends. After attending other meetings, and much hesitation, he invited home two Friends,—Thomas Carleton and Thomas Langhorn. Curiosity, and a report that he had turned Quaker, drew together all his neighbours; and Christopher Taylor, of Meggs Hill, William Graham, of Sikeside, and Francis Story, clerk and schoolmaster, of Kirklinton, submitted some written queries for the consideration of Carleton and Langhorn, which were discussed before the assembled neighbours, and a meeting was arranged to be held at Meggs Hill, on ground which is now the Friends' burial-ground at Hetherside, a spot which, to all Friends, must be hallowed ground, for there sleep many of their early preachers. These proceedings ended in the adhesion of Story, and some thirty more, to the Society of Friends. This was in 1672. Persecution immediately followed, and many were committed to the Sessions at Carlisle, where they had an unexpected escape from penalties; for the Sheriff arrested the informer, one Gilbert Atkinson, for debt. Atkinson was confined for many years, and died in prison, being supported there during the latter portion of his life by the very Friends against whom he had informed.

In 1677, Story began to travel as a preacher, or, as his journal terms it, "was called into the work of the ministry." He first visited Scotland. At a place which he calls Allassudin, he met a wealthy Friend, of the name of Walter Scott, an ancestor, we believe, of Sir Walter Scott. This Walter, however, left the Society. Story's next journey was to the dales of Yorkshire, to visit George Fox. He afterwards, in 1679, went, with John Banks, to the yearly meeting of Friends, in London; and accompanied Banks into the West of England. Story first made Banks's acquaintance at a meeting held at John Iveston's, at Jerishtoune.

The Society of Friends so prospered at Kirklinton, that Robert Priestman, the rector, frequently could only collect a congregation of five, and of his clerks three in succession were convinced, and left the church. The Friends now wished to build a meeting-house, and purchased wood for that purpose from Henry Dakers (Dacre;) but the Sessions at Carlisle, instigated by the Rector of Kirklinton, wrote to Dacre, who was a justice, and he would neither furnish the wood nor restore the money. The project of building a meeting-house thus fell to the ground, for all the wood was in the hands of great landowners, who declined to sell. Priest Priestman, who had stirred up the Sessions to action, died towards the end of the reign of Charles II. He was succeeded, as rector, by George Story, of Justus Town, who offered the Society, as a compromise, to let them alone, if they would not bring Friends from other parishes to their meetings. This proposal was rejected by the Friends, and the new rector immediately summoned them for "Sunday shillings," a fine imposed for not attending public worship; and his churchwarden indicted them at the Assizes, under the Popish Recusancy Act, which hit Quakers as well as Catholics. These intended severities failed for some time, as no one could be found to turn informer, until James Appleby, a stranger from Yorkshire, who had been educated for the law, and Christopher Story, of Allergarth, took on them that office, and laid an information before Justice Henry Forster, of Stonegarthside, against Christopher Story, of Righead, for attending a meeting of Friends. This attempt, also, failed; for the supposed offender was in Lancashire when the meeting was held. Appleby then laid another information before Justice Aglionby, of Drawdikes Castle, who issued his warrant to levy on Story's goods; but the constable, Richard Scott, was so sparing in making distress, that he was bound over, himself, to good behaviour in his office. When Story's goods were put up for sale, under the distress, no one would buy except the informer, Appleby. He made but little in his bargains; the wheat he purchased no one would or dare thresh; the sheep he bought were dispersed by all the sheep-dogs in Kirklinton parish, until he had but seven out of a large flock; and for two horses he could get no market nearer than Northumberland, and then only at half-prices. Highly enraged at his successive miscarriages, Appleby set off to London, and sued out subpœnas from Chief-Justice Jeffreys against sixteen of the Kirklinton Quakers, who, understanding a prison would be the result whether they obeyed the subpœnas or not, stayed at home. This contempt of the law seems to have been connived at by Justice Forster, who was unpleasantly recalled to a sense of his duty by being himself subpœnaed before the Chief-Justice, who happened to be coming the Northern Circuit, sent by the Court to bully the corporate towns into a surrender of their liberties and charters. Forster was brought before him at Carlisle, fined one hundred pounds, imprisoned, and deprived of his office of justice,—proceedings which dismayed the whole bench of justices. The Friends, however, all escaped, for the constables hid so, that Appleby could not get the warrants served until after the Assizes were over. Appleby and his son-in-law, George Waugh, again laid fresh informations before Justice Dacre, under which Christopher Story was fined twenty pounds, and several cows and young beasts were distrained; but the constables, when they put them up to sale, set men round to warn buyers off,—for which kindness to Story, one of them, George Irwin, got hauled up by the magistrates. Edward Atkinson, of Clift, and some other responsible men, also, went to Dacre, and got him to hold back the warrants over the winter. Meanwhile, Charles II. died, and the magistrates, who had been coerced by the fate of the late Justice Forster into severity against the Friends, at once declined to listen to Appleby, or to sell the goods taken under distress warrants. Story and others had, however, to appear at the Assizes, and were committed to prison, as they would not pay the prosecution fees. In prison, Story found John Banks and Thomas Hall, "in a dark place called the *Citydill*, among the Fellons, something like a Dungeon, where they could not see to Work in a Dark Day without Candle Light." Story escaped being put in here, as it was full. He was lodged in the gaoler's house, in Castle Street, until the gaoler, worn out by the persistence which Banks and his other captives exhibited in preaching, took another house. Story was released by King James's famous Proclamation of Indulgence. Under James II. the Friends ceased to be persecuted; even George Story, the Rector of Kirklinton, went without his tithes, rather than take legal proceedings for their recovery; the meetings of the Friends were unmolested, and, in consequence, they built a meeting-house at Sikeside, in Hethergill. This house was enlarged in 1699, and rebuilt in 1736. The wood, over which a difficulty had formerly occurred, was now procured from Scotland. Another small meeting-house was also built, north of the river

Line, which was difficult to cross in winter, there being neither bridge nor boat.

Thus, free from persecution, the Society now began to attack various abuses and evil practices. Among others, they opposed the old Cumberland custom (which has hardly now, some two hundred years later, died out) of making doles at burials. "That Practice," writes Story, "was grown so common, and to such an Extravagancy, that great Numbers of People came to burials, both Rich and Poor, without Invitation; and, as People were very extravagant in many things, this became a Snare to some, and an Uneasiness to us; and we could see no real Service in making such Doles, when People were met together on such a Weighty Occasion, but, on the contrary, great Disorders often happened. Thus we thought fit to break it off at once, which we did, and gave nothing at that Time to Poor or Rich; and, after a little time, the People saw it to be a good Way, and came from doing much to doing but a little; and People frequently came to our Burials, and that in a great deal of Seriousness,—scarce an high Word among them, . . . to the Satisfaction of Friends and others, so that I never yet heard of any Complaint for Want of outward Bread."

In 1687, Story visited the Friends in Ireland, and he also travelled to London, and as far as Bristol and the West, with John Boustead. In 1691, he travelled through Scotland, and visited Glasgow, where he found the people so barbarous, that he could not have supposed there were any such in the three nations. They burst into the house where he and his companions, Thomas Blain and James and John Milner, were, pulled the unoffending Friends out, and took them before the magistrates, who dismissed them, but abandoned them to the mercies of the rabble, by whom they were called Jesuits, spit upon, pelted with filth and stones, and chased far out of the town. The whole party contrived to get away unhurt. Story and his friends issued an address to the inhabitants of Glasgow, under the title of "A Looking-glass for the Inhabitants of the Town of Glasgow," in which they related the evil treatment they had met with there, compared Glasgow to Sodom, and prayed for the forgiveness of their persecutors. The next Friends that visited Glasgow had a mastiff set on them, so that the "Looking-glass" did not much mend matters.

Of the rest of his life, Story tells few, if any, particulars; but he continued to travel, visiting, at different times, England, Scotland, and Ireland. On many of his tours, his wife, who had now taken to public ministry, accompanied him; but he preserves no notes of his journeys. A warfare with James Armstrong, priest of Cannonby, occupies a good portion of the rest of the journal.

It began out of a meeting which Story appointed to be held at Broom Holm, on ground for which he had got permission from the owner. The opposition of Priest Armstrong induced the owner, at the last moment, to withdraw his permission, and the meeting was, in consequence, held on the highway, at Tarraside, about a mile from Cannonby Kirk. The Elders of the surrounding parishes appeared, accompanied by officers of the law and a disorderly mob; a riot ensued, in which John Boustead's head was broken until the blood ran down. The Friends, apparently, showed a moral fight of determination not to be driven away; for Story says: "A brave Warfare it was, and Friends kept their Places, old and young, and the Meeting continued near three Hours." For some years after this, no attempt was made by the Friends to invade Cannonby parish; but, in 1701, they held a meeting at Woodhouse Lees. Bailiff Melvin, with a strong party, both on horse and foot, tried to disperse the assembly, riding in among them as they sat on the ground. In the *mêlée*, some of the Friends were thrown down a steep place by way of dispersing them; some of the disturbers, also, were hurled over; the public Friends, or preachers, were dragged into a neighbouring wood, whither their congregation followed; Henry Atkinson, when he offered to pray, was dragged by two men on horseback through the river, where it was deep, and detained in a house on the other side. None of the party came to any injury; and Story afterwards wrote a letter to Priest Armstrong, of Cannonby, whom he regarded as the instigator of all this evil, in which he compares Armstrong and his brethren to all the persecutors that ever existed, from the inhabitants of Sodom down to the persecutors of the saints in New England. To this epistle, Armstrong made no reply, perhaps feeling himself unable to deal with such charges. He, however, interfered no more with meetings of Friends in his parish. This ends Story's journal, which comes only down to 1701. Story died in November, 1720, aged seventy-two, up to which time he continued to take a lead in the Society, and to travel. He was buried at the burial-ground at Hetherside. His wife survived until 1733, when she died, aged eighty-one.

In Story's journal, he records that, one Sunday, when the people were crossing the Esk, after attending worship at the Kirk of Cannonby, the boat suddenly sank, and, out of thirty-five passengers, twenty-eight were drowned, though the accident happened close to the bank. He gives no date to this, but it happened between 1693 and 1697.

In 1698, Story and his wife visited Scotland in October. The harvest was very backward, and at Aberdeen, they found the people reaping their corn, which had for a month been buried in snow. He says: "People made Fires in the Fields, it was so cold, which made both Corn and Fodder scarce. The poor People looked like Death; some dyed in the Highways, and more were supposed to dye with the Corn being unwholesome than for want of Bread."

Story's journal was published in 1726. It is a small book, of one hundred and forty-three pages, which contains, also, one or two letters to his wife and others, "An Epistle of Love and good Advice to the People of the Lord everywhere," and a few prefatory testimonies to his worth, by his wife, by Aaron Atkinson, Robert Latimer, and other friends, and a short conclusion by Latimer. Among his children, Story was, perhaps in consequence of the follies of his own youth, a strict disciplinarian, and, in one of his letters, gives orders that his sons are not to go out at night. Throughout his ministry of forty-three years, he took a leading part in the management of the Society's affairs, and was a great peacemaker among his friends and neighbours.

JOHN BOUSTEAD.

John Boustead was, in his day, a Friend of great reputation as a minister. He was born at Aglionby, near Carlisle, in the year 1659. We have little direct information about him, but he is mentioned in the journals of both Thomas and Christopher Story. Thomas Story's first tour as a preacher was taken in company with John Boustead. This journey took place in 1692. Boustead and Story met, by agreement, at Healy Hall, near Newcastle, and, after attending several meetings there, proceeded, by Morpeth and Kelso to Edinburgh, where they fell in with one Thomas Rudd, a Leicestershire miller, and a preacher of much enthusiasm, who had been traversing the streets and colleges of Edinburgh, crying out "Woe to the sandy foundation!" Rudd is described as "having a voice suited to the measure of his words, with an innocent boldness in his countenance, frequently lifting his right hand towards heaven as he passed along, which was with a slow and grave pace." With Rudd, Boustead and his companion went to make some farewell visits, after the conclusion of the Quarterly Meeting, which they had come to attend at Edinburgh. Rudd felt suddenly moved again to cry through the street. Boustead and Story suffered him to go alone, not feeling called upon to hazard their lives or liberties by meddling in his concerns; but, after they had waited his return for some time, they set out to seek for him. Rudd was discovered in a low shop in the old High Street of Edinburgh, where he had been thrust by the rabble. Boustead, who was a bold, able-bodied man, not to say a fighting Quaker, pressed through the mob, and pulled Rudd out, to a stone by the town-cross, from which post Rudd began to give forth his warnings, under protection of Boustead. Some of the crowd that soon gathered mocked the party, and pelted them with a pack of old playing-cards; others were more serious, and wondered what could make Rudd and his friends so daring. A report got into circulation, that Rudd was "he who went through London with a message, and shortly after there was an earthquake there." So great was the excitement stirred up, that the bailies called out several companies of soldiers, and drew them up over against the Tolbooth, and Rudd was taken before the chief bailie, Charles Charteris, who committed him to the Tolbooth. In the evening, Boustead got admission into that prison, and found himself and Rudd great objects of curiosity to the prisoners, among whom there were many Episcopalians, who had been rioting on account of the suppression of their clergy. Another singular view of the prison system of the age, is afforded us by the account of Rudd's imprisonment, and Boustead's visit to him. We hear of the Common Hall of the prison, and of the "Quaker's High Room," an apartment of deal, which the Friends had made in "time of greater persecution, for their own convenience." Here, Rudd and his visitors supped, and the Episcopalian prisoners were much gratified to note that they craved a blessing before their meat. After supper, Boustead returned to his lodgings. Next day, he attacked Chief-Bailie Charteris as he came out of his court, and told him, with great boldness, that it would "be a great reflection on the Presbyterians in Scotland, who so lately themselves had been hardly used, as they said, by the Episcopalians," to begin persecuting the Friends. Boustead's boldness carried the day, and Rudd was released. The three, after visiting some ladies of high rank in Edinburgh, travelled round Scotland, going as far as Aberdeen and Inverness. Rudd and Boustead preached at all the towns they came to. Sometimes the people and the audience were friendly, sometimes the reverse; but at Glasgow and Hamilton, and particularly the latter place, they were mobbed, and fared very badly.

We have little more to relate of Boustead. He has been mentioned, in an account of Christopher Story, as being present, and having his head broke, at disturbances which arose when the Friends attempted to hold meetings in Cannonby parish; and he also visited Ireland, at some time or other, in company with George Rooke. He died in 1716, and was buried at Scotby.

AARON, HENRY, AND JOSEPH ATKINSON.

AARON, HENRY, and JOSEPH ATKINSON, three brothers, were the sons of a couple of Friends of that name, who lived at Masthorn, in the parish of Stapleton, and about four or five miles from Righead. Both their parents died early, leaving six small children, of whom Aaron is said to have been born in 1665. The children were distributed among their relations, to be brought up, and thus Aaron, being placed with Presbyterians, became a Presbyterian, while Joseph and Henry, for similar reasons, joined the Church of England. Henry was apprenticed to a tailor in Newcastle, and afterwards moved to London, where he continued that trade. He lived there for fourteen years. While in London, he joined the Friends, and became a preacher. He then settled in Cumberland, but visited Scotland and Ireland several times; and finally died at Banbury, of fever and ague, as he was returning from a preaching tour in the South of England. He was then aged about sixty, and had been a preacher for about thirty years; but neither the date of his birth nor death is to be found in the authorities we have consulted. Henry Atkinson was present at one of the stormy meetings of Friends held in the parish of Cannonby, when Bailiff Melvin interfered; and on that occasion, Henry Atkinson was dragged through the river Esk by two men on horseback. Of Joseph Atkinson little is recorded, except that he left the Church of England, and joined the Society of Friends, on arriving at manhood. He did not travel much, but, still, he visited meetings in Scotland. He died in the year 1738, at his house at Righead, aged about sixty-four, and was buried at Hetherside. Aaron, the third son, was apprenticed to William Armstrong, and was a packman, and carried a linen pack on his back. While on his rounds, he stayed with a relative, William Graham, of Sikeside, and was by him taken to a meeting of Friends at the house of Christopher Taylor. Here, "he was," writes Christopher Story, "as one slain at once, and freely giving up, went out in the Faith, and greatly prevailed." Armstrong, his master, was at first inclined to get rid of Aaron after his conversion, but, on second thoughts, determined to make further trial of him. In the end, Armstrong, also, was converted, and became a Friend. He and his apprentice used to attend meetings, and preached together, and drew very large audiences, even of people who were not

Friends. They prospered, too, in business, which, at first, after their conversion, declined, but afterwards revived, as they were found to be honest in their dealings. Christopher Story says of them: "And though they lived near Scotland, yet they saw they were not to trade in goods which were prohibited, as many did; neither were they free to sell such striped or gaudy cloth as was not seemly for Friends to wear." Most of the Border packmen of that day knew, we fancy, many of the old moss-troopers' paths into Scotland, and were not averse to a little smuggling.

Aaron, after a time, gave up his business, and extended his travels as a preacher, not only throughout England, Scotland, and Ireland, but also to America, where he met Thomas Story, of Justus Town, and travelled in company with him. Returning to England, he settled at Leeds, and died at his own house, in 1740.

Christopher Atkinson, of Westmorland, may possibly have been a member of this family. We know little of his history. He was imprisoned, on account of his religious opinions, both at Kendal and at Norwich. He afterwards left the Society, through a scandal he brought on it by an intrigue with a maid servant. While he remained in the Society, he wrote several small essays in defence of their tenets, and then he used to subscribe with the following formula: "By one whose name in the flesh is Christopher Atkinson, who am one that the world doth scornfully call a Quaker." While Christopher Atkinson was in Kendal Gaol, one John Gilpin, of that place, who had been a Friend, apostatised, and published a book, called "The Quaker Shaken," in defence of his apostacy. To this, Christopher Atkinson replied, in a production entitled "An Answer to the 'Quaker Shaken,' by one John Gilpin, wherein is discovered his Life, and how the Judgment of God was and is upon him, and how he hath been led by Deceit and Filthiness to Blaspheme the Name of the Living God, and is returned with the Dog to the Vomit, and with the Sow to her Wallowing." Edward Burrough wrote a Preface to this, which was signed by the following Friends, then prisoners in Kendal Gaol: Miles Halhead, Thomas Holmes, Thomas Casley, Alice Wilson, Agnes Turner, Margaret Newby, Mary Collinson, Jane Waugh, Dorothy Waugh, Mary Hougil, Elizabeth Levens, Elizabeth Bateman, Mary Warrener, and Margaret Gilpin. This Atkinson was a man of unbridled tongue, and once, if not oftener, was cast into prison for libelling and slandering his opponents, particularly an attorney at Warwick.

PETER AND JANE FEARON.

In our account of John Banks, of Brigham, we mentioned that he had an apprentice, Peter Fearon, of Seaton, to whom he addressed some of his epistles. This Peter was originally a member of the Church of England, but left that body, and, like his master, became a minister among the Friends, and travelled, not only through England and Scotland, but even through Germany and Holland, being the companion of many of the Society's most celebrated preachers. He lived to the good old age of eighty-four, and died in November, 1734. His wife, Jane, who died in September, 1737, aged eighty-two, was for fifty years a preacher, and was also the writer of a few papers on the tenets of the Society of Friends.

Peter Fearon is described as "an able minister, sound in doctrine, convincing to gainsayers, confirming and edifying to the Churches; very serviceable in meetings for discipline, and zealously concerned therein for providing good order, being particularly gifted for that good work."

THOMAS STORDY.

THOMAS STORDY, of Moorhouse, was born to the inheritance of an handsome estate, and, at an early age, joined the Society of Friends. In the year 1662, he was at Carlisle during the Assizes, and went to visit some of his friends and acquaintances who were in prison there. He was illegally detained in custody by the gaoler, and on the following morning brought up before Judge Turner. Nothing could be proved against him; indeed, nothing was laid to his charge; but the common trap for all members of the Society of Friends was set for him,—he was tendered the oath of allegiance, and on his refusing, from conscientious objections, to swear at all, he was subjected to the penalty of a premunire. Under the premunire, the Sheriff of Cumberland, John Lowther, seized and sold, at prices far below their value, all Stordy's real and personal estate; and Stordy himself was detained a prisoner in Carlisle Gaol for ten years, at the expiration of which time he was set at liberty. His real estate was restored to him, at the intercession of the Earl of Carlisle. A few years after his release, he was prosecuted under an obsolete Act of Parliament, and fined twenty pounds a month, for absenting himself from public worship. He was thrown into prison, and died there in 1684, after a second confinement of several years.

Sewell, in his History of the Friends, describes his death thus:—

"Not long before his decease, he exhorted those that were come to visit him to faithfulness. 'For,' said he, 'if ye continue faithful to the Lord whilst ye live in this world, he will reward you, as now he rewardeth me, with his sweet peace.' Thus piously Thomas Stordy departed this life, showing forth that he was really a gentleman, whose chiefest nobility consisted in virtue."

During his life, he released, by deed to the landowners and their heirs for ever, an impropriation of ten pounds per annum for hay-tithes, which had descended to him from his grandfather and father,—"making conscience as well of receiving as of paying tithes."

No exact record of his family is to be found, but descendants of his are now living in and near Carlisle. He was uncle to the David Hodgson whom we mention next; and a daughter of his married George Bewley, son of Mungo Bewley, of Carlisle.

DAVID HODGSON AND JONATHAN OSTELL.

DAVID HODGSON was born in 1676, at Wormanby, near Moorhouse, in Cumberland. He was a nephew of Thomas Stordy, of Moorhouse, and his parents were persons of good repute, who gave him a religious education. Little is put on record of his life. He first took to public ministry, as a Friend, in 1704, or, as the quaint old book from which we gather our information says, "came forth in a public Testimony to the Universality of the Love of God in Christ Jesus, and to the effectual Operation of his Grace in the Hearts and Souls of Mankind, in order to their Salvation; and his Ministry was attended with a fervent engagement of Spirit for the Cause of Truth, and the Prosperity thereof." He attended several of the yearly meetings of the Society of Friends in London, and also travelled through Scotland and Ireland as a preacher. He died in the year 1755, of paralysis, by which his mental faculties were somewhat impaired, and was buried in the Friends' burying-ground at Moorhouse.

David Hodgson is recorded in the annals of the Society as "a loving Husband, a kind Friend, a peaceable Neighbour, and charitable to the Poor and Afflicted."

With David Hodgson's name we have coupled that of his friend and neighbour, JONATHAN OSTELL, of Moorhouse. Jonathan was born one year later than David,—namely, in 1677. His parents were persons of good esteem among Friends, who gave him a sober and religious education. As he grew up, he found his mind strongly inclined to the customs and fashions of the world, but he resisted, and "witnessed a happy change in himself," and became an able minister of the Gospel, visiting, on several occasions, the Friends' meetings in England, Scotland, and Ireland.

Jonathan Ostell died in 1752, aged seventy-seven, and was buried at Moorhouse. For a few years before his death, he was very infirm, and had lost his sight; but he travelled up to London in his seventy-fourth year, to attend the Annual Meeting of the Society, to which he and his friend Hodgson were often delegated together by the Friends in Cumberland, as their representatives. Their names also occur together in the journal of Thomas Story, who used to attend meetings at Moorhouse, and stay with one or other of the two.

Both Hodgson and Ostell demonstrated the sincerity of their conscientious scruples against tithes in the same manner as Thomas Story: not only did they object to pay them, but to receive them. Both were the owners of impropriate tithes, which during their lives they declined to receive payment of; and both, by their wills, devised the tithes of which they were impropriators to the owners of the estates out of which they were payable.

JAMES DICKENSON.

JAMES DICKENSON, of Greentrees, a fellmonger by trade, was born at Lowmoor House, in the parish of Dean, in the year 1658. His parents were Matthew and Jane Dickenson, who brought him up religiously; but his mother died when he was seven, and his father when he was ten years old. At first, Dickenson took to youthful pleasures; but, giving them up, he appears to have got the reputation of being a Quaker before he really was one. His mind, however, was in an unsettled state. In 1678, he presented himself at a Presbyterian meeting at Tallentire, and was forcibly ejected, but, standing outside of the window, delivered a short address to the congregation within; in return for which they came out, bumped his head on the stones, and dragged him down the street. A similar scene occurred when he visited a meeting of Baptists at Broughton. Noways daunted, he returned to Tallentire again, and bearded the Presbyterian priest, George Larcum, or Larkham, (who had been parson of Cockermouth during the Commonwealth,) in his own house. Dickenson was again ejected, and Mrs. Larcum threatened him with the stocks.

A year or two later on, in 1680, Dickenson commenced to travel as a preacher, going round Westmorland, the Yorkshire dales, the Bishoprick of Durham, and Northumberland. In 1682, he went to Ireland with Thomas Wilson. For some years he travelled round England, Scotland, Wales, and Ireland, and then went to Germany and Holland with Peter Fearon. On the voyage, they had a narrow escape of being captured by a Turkish privateer. After some years of travelling, he went with Thomas Wilson to Barbadoes. After a few days' sail, the French fleet of sixty sail bore down upon the English fleet of merchantmen, which was under convoy, and captured the whole of them, except three, the ships in which the Friends were escaping under a friendly fog. Near Barbadoes, what was supposed to be a French privateer hove in sight. The English crew was called to quarters, and the captain ordered Wilson and Dickenson, as they would not fight, to go below with the doctor. They declined, and took up an exposed position on the quarter-deck, saying, it was conscience, and not cowardice, that prevented them from fighting. The alarm was, however, a false one. From Barbadoes, the two went to America, and visited the Friends there, going through many adventures, and running considerable dangers from the Indians, from French, from wild beasts, and from floods. Returning to Barbadoes, they were there during a dangerous plot by the negroes to kill all the whites, which was luckily frustrated.

Dickenson returned from abroad in 1693, and married a young woman of Pardshaw, but went on a second visit to America in 1695. He records that there were several priests on board the vessel with him, who were going out to Maryland, having heard that a tax of forty pounds of tobacco per head was to be levied for the advancement of their wages. He returned from America in 1697, with a convoy of one hundred and thirty sail, who had to go far to the southward to avoid the French fleet. During the voyage a storm arose, which created great confusion in the fleet, one ship being driven into another; and Dickenson's ship sprung a leak, and nearly foundered. Dickenson afterwards made a third visit to America, 1713–1715, when Thomas Wilson was again his companion. They sailed from Whitehaven in a vessel of which Richard Kelsick was master,—a man of whom Dickenson writes in the highest terms. Their return voyage was a dangerous one; they nearly foundered, and with difficulty got back to port. While in England, he travelled much as a minister, but his journal ceases soon after his final return from America, for, being paralysed, he could not write. His wife died in 1726. He survived until 1741, and was buried at Eaglesfield.

THOMAS WILSON.

THOMAS WILSON was of Soulby, in Dacre parish. He writes: "My parents' names were Edward and Ann Wilson, who brought me up in the profession of the Church of England, and taught me the Catechism, having been sprinkled or baptised in my infancy, according to the manner of that Church." He became a Friend, and was the companion of James Dickenson on the first and last of his American visits. He died in 1724. Many of this name were ministers among the Society of Friends,—such as Christopher Wilson, of Greysouthen; Rachel and Deborah Wilson, of Kendal.

THOMAS STORY.

THOMAS STORY, of Justus Town, near Carlisle, was as genuine a Cumberland worthy as ever lived. Our information is taken from his journal, a ponderous folio of nigh eight hundred pages, published in 1747,—a book which once fell, by accident, into the hands of the late Lord Brougham, and with which he was so charmed as to spend a whole Sunday, during the Lancaster Assizes, in its perusal. The greater part, however, of the book is taken up with long disquisitions on religious points, unsuited for our quotation; but we shall endeavour to select what will most interest our readers.

Thomas Story was born at Justice Town, in the Parish of Kirklinton, probably between 1660 and 1670. His father owned property there, which Story afterwards purchased from the widow of one of his brothers, and which now belongs to Captain Irwin, of Calder Abbey. His elder brother was chaplain to the Earl of Carlisle, and incumbent of Kirklinton; he appears to have been an ar chaplain, in King William's army in Irela was afterwards, in succession, Dean of Conn Limerick. The journal gives us but little info tion about Story's education, except that he was at school in Carlisle, and was playmate there with the third Earl of Carlisle, then a boy under the care of his grandfather, the first Earl. Story was intended for the law; but, before he commenced to study for his profession, his father sent him to the "Fencing School, as a fashionable and manly accomplishment." He was afterwards placed to read law "under a counsellor in the country." This was Counsellor Gilpin, son of "Dr. Richard Gilpin, of Scaleby Castle, in Cumberland, a famous and learned physician, and also a superintendent among that people, (the Presbyterians,) in Oliver's days." The counsellor then resided in the country, apparently in the West of Cumberland, near Whitehaven, where he afterwards settled and became a justice of the peace. In 1687, Story and the counsellor came out of the country, and had chambers in the city of Carlisle. Carlisle at that time was held by a strong garrison in the interest of James II., commanded by officers who were mostly Papists and Irishmen. From other sources, we learn that the Corporation (a body then most completely under the control of James, who had just weeded out of it Sir Christopher Musgrave and Sir George Fletcher) made nine of these Papist and Irish officers honorary, or "mushroom," freemen of the city. The liberty of the citizens was a good deal curtailed by the military power. For instance, when John Scansfield, — a noted Quaker, though by many suspected to be a Jesuit, preached one Sunday, in 1688, in the Town Hall, musketeers were placed as sentinels at the door, and many of the officers attended,—precautions in whose absence, the good citizens would have probably by force prevented either Quaker or Papist from giving tongue in that ancient place. In the same year, too, the military appear to have celebrated, with great orgies, the news that a Prince of Wales (the old Pretender) was born. They made a great bonfire in the Market-place, "where they drank wine, till, with that and the transport of the news, they were exceedingly distracted, throwing their hats into the fire at one health, their coats at the next, their waistcoats at a third, and so on to their shoes; and some of them threw in their shirts, and then ran about naked, like madmen." When the time of trial came, those enthusiastic warriors hardly rose equal to the occasion, for no sooner did they hear of the arrival of the Prince of Orange, than they stole away from Carlisle in the night, thus enabling Sir John Lowther and the Protestant gentry of the country to secure the town, and cut off the retreat of General Clavers, (Viscount Dundee,) who had just passed through Cumberland, to aid King James, with a force of about three thousand horse and foot, calling at Lowther on Sir John, on his way south.

Story himself, at the time, nearly got into a scrape; for he wrote an account of how the Revolution progressed at Carlisle, to his brother, then chaplain to the Dowager Countess of Carlisle, and with her at Castle Howard. The letter was intercepted, and fell into the hands of Lord Delamere, who commanded the partisans of the Prince of Orange in the North. Some of the sentiments in the letter gave offence, and Story got a hint, through his brother, that he was to be more careful in future. Story's mind was at this time beginning to turn towards the consideration of religious matters, and to develop that taste and ability for discussing them, of which we find so many traces in his journal. The earliest discussion he puts on record is one which took place at an Assize dinner, at an inn in Carlisle, where were present, besides Story, two ministers of the Church of England, and "a Popish gentleman, who moved a debate concerning transubstantiation." The two ministers were by no means anxious to enter on the subject; but Story took it up, and lectured the ministers soundly on their backwardness. It is impossible, within the limits of this notice, to give any account of the theological views which Story, in various arguments of great ability, advances. Mainly, they are those of the Society of Friends, to whom he shortly after this joined himself. He was ready, on all occasions, to have a religious discussion with any opponent, and generally entered a full account of his argument in his journal, to which we must refer those who care for more than a few biographical notes about this remarkable man. Story, in alluding to worldly temptations which surrounded him, describes himself when a young man, thus :—

> "The airs of youth were many and potent; strength, activity, and comeliness of person were not awanting, and had their share; nor were natural endowments of mind, or competent acquirements, afar off; and the glory, advancements, and preferments of the world, spread as nets in my view; and the friendship thereof beginning to address me with flattering courtship. I wore a sword, which I well understood, and had foil'd several masters of that science in the north and at London; and rode with firearms also, of which I knew the use; and yet I was not quarrelsome; for though I emulated, I was not envious."

He adds, that he was always determined to resent and punish an affront, or personal injury, when it was done "in contempt, or with design;" but goes on to tell us that he "never met with any, save once; and then I kept to my own maxims with success; and yet so as neither to wound nor be wounded." Hence, we fancy, he fought a duel with swords, and disarmed his opponent. An accident, by which the neck of his horse was broke, as he was riding one Sunday to some church in the country, appears to have occasioned his complete weaning from the world, and set him upon very serious consideration of religious questions. He withdrew from attending at church, but joined, as yet, no other sect.

"Outwardly, (he writes,) I put off my usual airs, my jovial actions and address, and laid aside my sword, which I had worn, not through design of injury, nor fear of any, but as a modish and manly ornament. I burnt also my instruments of music, and divested myself of the superfluous parts of my apparel, retaining only that which was necessary, or deemed decent."

At this time, Story had his extraordinary dreams, or rather visions, one of which he describes thus:—

"There appeared a city, near the gates whereof stood the fairest house therein, which was high and magnificent, into which a man of low stature seemed about to enter. He was habited as a post, or carrier of a Prince, bringing great and swift commands and news, with a trumpet in his right hand, transparent as fine polished crystal, and without wrinkle or wreath, and therewith he sounded towards the north with a strong, constant, equal, and inarticulate voice, and the breath of his mouth issuing through it was as a flame of fire, in form of a two-edged sword. Having finished his sounding towards the north, he took the trumpet from his mouth, and held it in his right hand, with his arm stretched towards the east, and his face still towards the north, with his eyes intent towards heaven, his right ear turned upward, reclining towards the east, his mouth a little open, and his breath glowing therefrom as a lambent flame; and as one hearkening, with deep attention, for fresh orders from the King of Kings. But I looked unto himself alone; and, in the twinkling of an eye, he set the trumpet to his mouth again, with majesty and zeal, and, turning it toward the earth, the breath of his mouth therethrough was as a stream of fire and brimstone, which pierced the earth, drove it hither and thither, and melted the stones before him. The city was then alarmed, and pale death appeared on every face; the gay of this world were astonished, and the mighty thereof in war trembled in great amazement and fear, but knew not where to hide themselves."

This was in 1689–1690, when Story appears to have been deeply imbued with religious enthusiasm. He thought much upon religious matters; and the highly imaginative tone of his mind led him to see visions, and, occasionally, to be thrown into a sort of trance, in which "silence was commanded in him," and which generally terminated in his writing a long religious rhapsody, of high poetical merit, many of which are preserved in his journal. He did not, as we have before said, as yet join any sect; but he attended worship at St. Cuthbert's, as its service was not celebrated with "that pomp, show, and noise as at the Cathedral." Religious doubts, however, at last threw his mind into such trouble and darkness, that he withdrew from attendance on any form of worship, in which state he remained until about the end of 1690, when he was seized with an inclination to inquire into the way and principles of the Society of

Friends. The opportunity of doing so was offered him in May, 1691. He was staying at an inn in the west of Cumberland, kept by a Friend, by whom he was taken to a meeting at Broughton. The proceedings at this meeting affected Story so much as to attract universal notice. The Society welcomed him as a convert, and invited him to meet the "Ministering Friend" at the house of Widow Hall, in Broughton; and he afterwards dined with Richard Ribton, "an ancient and honourable Friend in the village."

Story returned to Carlisle, where the innkeeper invited him, and persuaded him, to go to a great meeting of Friends, about four miles from that city. At this meeting, disputes ran high on the subject of the discipline of the Society; and, as Story had not yet professed himself a Friend, he got a hint to withdraw. His indecision in the matter was terminated by his being requested to appear as a witness to the signature of some deeds which he had drawn (he had been practising as a conveyancer in Carlisle) for a friend of his, one Thomas Tod. Rather than take an oath, Story examined well his feelings, and, as the result, avowed himself a Friend. Tod, who was much disgusted at the idea of losing his cause through any religious doubts on Story's part, threatened him with fine and imprisonment; but, his adversary yielding, he won his cause without requiring

Story's testimony. This happened at the Assizes at Carlisle, in 1691, when the city was unusually full of people, and Story found himself an object of universal curiosity. Some came to stare at him; some bowed low unto him, to see if he would bow in return; others grinned and scoffed; and some, who dare not have done so before he professed the doctrines of the Society of Friends, insulted him. Story's position, his abilities and learning both as a lawyer and scholar, made his conversion remarkable; and it appears to have made much stir, both in the city and the county. It was, by some, proposed to have a general meeting of the clergy, to try and re-convert him,—a proposal which fell through, from the lukewarmness of the clergy, who rather shunned Story. It is, indeed, probable that, in both learning and polemics, he was more than a match for the local ministers, and that they knew it. Others, and among them his father, tried to get him to a tavern, to drink a hearty glass, with a view of raising his spirits into a more sociable temper; they got him there, and then proposed the King, which toast Story refused to drink, and the meeting broke up, all parting good friends, but rather having their spirits reduced to his level, than his raised to theirs. Dr. Gilpin tried argument, but failed, after which Story was let alone. His father even became reconciled to his son's conversion, by the thought that, as the

Friends were an opulent people, and involved in many lawsuits about tithes, his son might do well as a lawyer among them. Story cut this hope short, by declining to practise, much to his father's disgust. The old gentleman then seems to have comforted himself with an erroneous idea that the Friends paid their ministers, and that his son would succeed in that line.

Story, within a very short time after joining the Society of Friends, commenced going the circuits of their meetings. His first journey was round Northumberland and Yorkshire, returning by the west of Cumberland, where he attended meetings at Cockermouth, Broughton, Allonby, and Longnewton. About the end of 1692, he joined with John Boustead and Thomas Rudd, and went a tour round Scotland, where the party made the acquaintance of the Tolbooth at Edinburgh for creating a disturbance, by preaching, in the High Street. At Aberdeen, and at Elgin, they got into collision with the military authorities, and at the latter place were lodged in the guard-house. They went as far north as Inverness, where they addressed the Highlanders, and also several of the officers of the garrison, who were friendly, unlike the gentlemen of their cloth at Elgin and Aberdeen. At Hamilton, they were mobbed by Cameronians, who ill-used them much, pelting them with dirt, beating them, and making an attempt to duck Rudd in a well. In the following year, Story was appointed, with John Banks, of Brigham, to represent the Cumberland Friends, in the yearly meeting of the Society, in London. After his return, he came to a resolution to leave his father, who was still much vexed with his son's defection from the law. Rather, however, than part with him, the old gentleman was willing to make over all his property to him. Story declined this offer, and again went up to London; and, after a tour among the Friends in the West of England, settled there, in 1695, as a conveyancer. Through the interest of William Penn, whose warm friend he became, Story soon acquired a very large business, which he did not push so far as he might have done, for fear it should become a hindrance to him in the ministry. In London he continued to reside for some time, though he was frequently absent on long tours to attend meetings, visiting Ireland in company with William Penn, and also Scotland. While he was resident in London, Peter the Great visited England. Story, with another Friend, named Mollyson, called at the Czar's lodgings, in York Buildings, on pretence of inquiring about a cousin of Mollyson, who had been in Russia, in the Czar's service. They saw the Czar and Prince Menzicoff, (*sic*, in Story's journal,) and had a long discourse with him, through an interpreter, by whose means the Czar inquired, when he learnt his visitors were Friends, "Of what use can you be in any kingdom or Government, seeing you will not bear arms and fight?" At the conclusion of their interview, they presented Peter with two Latin copies of Barclay's "Apology for Quakerism," and declined some gold which he offered as payment. The Czar returned the visit by appearing suddenly with Menzicoff at a Friends' meeting in Gracechurch Street.

In 1698, Story carried out an intention he had long had of visiting Pennsylvania. This project was much opposed by his father; but still Story persisted, and in September, 1698, he sailed from Gravesend in the good ship Providence, of London, William Penn himself being among the company that came to see Story off. After a stormy voyage of about three months, they arrived in Chesapeake Bay. At one of the first places he visited, he found a priest of the English Church who was paid according to the work he did,—a hogshead of tobacco for each sermon. As the unfortunate man was paralysed, and could not preach, he had had no pay for some years. Story settled in Pennsylvania, and was appointed William Penn's deputy in the province, and also a member of the Council of State, Keeper of the Great Seal, Master of the Rolls, and one of the Commissioners of Property. He married, in 1706, Ann Shippen, the daughter of Edward Shippen, a member of the

Society of Friends, who left England in 1675, and made a large fortune as a merchant in Philadelphia. He was Speaker of the House of Assembly, and also the first Mayor of that town,—an honour to which Story was afterwards elected, but which he declined. She died in 1711 or 1712.

Story's journal contains many interesting accounts of society and manners in America, and of the dangers the settlers incurred from Indians, into which we have not room to go. In November, 1708–9, he paid a visit to Barbadoes, Antigua, Jamaica, and other of the Western Isles; and was captured by a French privateer, and carried to Port-a-pee, in Hispaniola, where Story availed himself of his knowledge of Latin to hold theological arguments with the Jesuit priests. He was afterwards taken by the privateer to Guadaloupe, and endured great sufferings on the voyage; but from that place he got a passage back to Antigua, and thence to Pennsylvania.

In 1714, he left Pennsylvania, and returned to England, visiting Barbadoes and Antigua *en route*. His first visit, after his return, was to William Penn, whom he found in almost a childish state, from the effects of an apoplectic fit. He then travelled northwards, attending meetings on his way, and finally arrived at Justice Town, where he found his father still alive, but quite blind. Story only stayed with his father for about ten days, and then set off again southwards. He visited Wigton on his way, where some persons of the name of Robinson, and also Job and Lot Pearson, Ranters, apparently apostate Quakers, interrupted the meetings. The wife of one of the Robinsons abused Story at the funeral of a Quaker's child, and was by him treated, not to his usual weapon, a theological argument, but to the threat "of a ducking-stool, or a few good rods at the tail of a cart, as a common scold." Story went on to Whitehaven, to see his old friends, two of the Gilpins, sons of Dr. Richard Gilpin, one a councillor and justice of the peace, and the other a merchant. Continuing his journey, he came to Oxford, where he fell in for riots, in which the Presbyterian and Quaker meeting-houses were wrecked by a mob of the scholars and others, and some Quaker houses damaged. This mischief was a concomitant of the general election of 1715, done in revenge for a proposal made by "the Low party" at Oxford to burn the pictures of the Queen and Dr. Sacheverill. At this election the Quakers had voted with the Low or Whig party. From Oxford, Story went to London, and thence to Yarmouth, and there embarked for a tour through Holland, Friezland, and Germany, to visit the continental Friends, who were allied to a foreign religious society, whose members were called Menists. Returning to Yarmouth, he visited the Gurneys at Norwich. For several years, up to

1740 or 1741, Story continued to travel round to the Quaker meetings in England, Ireland, and Scotland, though latterly he stayed a good deal at Justice Town, having purchased his father's property from the widow of his elder brother. There he built a house, and planted a nursery of forest trees. "Oaks, elms, ashes, acer-majors, poplars of several kinds, firs, English walnuts, black walnuts, tulip-trees, locust-trees, cedars of America, occidental planes, lindels, chesnuts, horse-chesnuts, divers sorts of willows, beeches, hornbeans, scarlet oaks, &c., which I had raised from seeds and cuttings after their several kinds at that farm, to furnish that part of the country, in time, with timber, which is now scarce, and that I might be an example to others in that useful kind of improvement, which several since have begun to follow." Story's plantations remain at the present day, and one or more of the tulip trees still flower annually. It has been suggested to the writer, by a member of the Society of Friends well acquainted with the fine woods at Castle Howard, that Story had a good deal to do with their planting. He was a playmate, in youth, of the Earl of Carlisle who built Castle Howard, and planted the woods; this acquaintance was renewed on Story's return from Pennsylvania; he frequently visited Castle Howard, informed the Earl of the boundless forests he had seen in America, and was doubtless, as a practical planter of trees, consulted by the Earl.

Towards the close of his life, Story had two paralytic strokes, which disabled him greatly. He died at Justice Town, in 1742, and was buried in in the Friends' burial-ground at Carlisle. The following account of him appeared in the *London Daily Advertiser*, of June 28th, 1743:—

"On Monday, the 21st of June, 1742, Died, of a Paralytick Disorder, at Carlisle, aged about eighty, Mr. Thomas Story, an eminent Preacher among the Quakers; a man justly esteemed and lov'd, not only by that Society, but by many of others, not of the meanest rank, who had the pleasure of his acquaintance. He was truly a great and good man, whose principles led him to the performance of every moral and Christian Duty, and whose life and doctrines concurred in rendering him a fit example for Gospel Ministers, in Wisdom, Piety, and Humility. He had, without any professed application to Sciences, acquired a general Knowledge in Natural Philosophy, and most branches of the Mathematicks, and had the most refined and extensive Ideas in the Metaphysicks; but the inward and eternal happiness of Mankind was his favourite study. He was a Complete Gentleman, generous in his sentiments, affable in his behavior, free and communicative to people in all stations and circumstances. His time was chiefly devoted to the service of God, in discharging that public concern of Preaching the Gospel, which he esteemed his indispensable duty; of the good effect of whose extraordinary and faithful labours there are many living Witnesses. In short, if Temperance, Patience, Forgiving Injuries, Humility, Faith, and Charity are Characteristics of a Good Man and a Minister of Christ, he was one."

Story left funds for the publication of his journal, which is, in the main, a record of tours to attend meetings of the Society of Friends. The book is one which well repays perusal, though Story kept out of it much interesting matter that he might well have inserted. He was a proficient in natural science, and must in his travels have seen many curious things; yet he excludes from his journal all such, and also all the important public business he was concerned in. Of his own private affairs he says little; he never hints that he was married. Many odd facts are to be gleaned out of Story's journal, which illustrate the social life of the times in which he lived. For instance, it would appear that both Lord Carlisle and Lord Lonsdale, whom he used to visit, dined in the middle of the day, and had supper about the present dinner hour. The gaol system of the time is brought home to us very oddly, by an account of how the Governor of Carlisle Gaol, in 1707, allowed prisoners to go out to interrupt meetings of Friends,—a nuisance which the Governor of the city abated by the help of a corporal and a file of musketeers; and a curious picture is presented to us by a note,—that at one meeting, a doctor of divinity was rumoured to be present, disguised in a blue coat. There were, in those days, penalties against attending meetings of dissenters, which Justice Appleby, of Kirklinton, and his wife, are mentioned as on one occasion running the hazard of. An odd expression that occurs in the journal is, "Threepenny curates," whom Story explains to be poor clergymen who "say prayers for the richer sort for threepence a-time, which is paid twopence in farthings and a dish of coffee." We have been told that the late Earl of Carlisle, in reply to a question sent him by letter, said he had read Story's journal, a copy of which is at Castle Howard, and that the dignified conversation recorded there, between Henry, Viscount Lonsdale, and Story, had much modified his sentiments regarding the Society of Friends, and their opposition to the payment of ecclesiastical demands.

Story was a man of high social position, both by birth and by learning. He was Greek scholar enough to put Dr. Bradford, Bishop of Carlisle, in a hole, by that prelate's own confession, over the Greek text of the New Testament. He visited, as we have mentioned, Lords Carlisle and Lowther at their seats; while Dean Tullie, of Carlisle, "Old Counsellor Aglionby," the Recorder of that city, and Richard Aglionby, the Registrar, are mentioned in the journal as his kind and old friends. With William Penn he was very intimate.

Story took an active part, after his return from America, in an agitation to get the Friends relieved from a form of affirmation to which they much objected. Indeed, he himself suffered an imprisonment of over a year for declining to make the obnoxious affirmation. In this agitation, the Earl of Carlisle helped him greatly, and, at a reception at his town house, in Dover Street, introduced Story to the Earl of Sunderland, with whom Story had a long conversation on the subject. He also visited the Duke of Somerset, the Archbishops of Canterbury and York, and the Bishop of Carlisle, to ask for their assistance, and was received by all most kindly. Of Dawes, Archbishop of York, Story writes:—"He had as much of the gentleman as Bishop in him, and the former seemed rather predominant." Story's efforts were at last successful.

Thomas Story was an intimate friend of James Logan, secretary to William Penn, and Chief-Justice of Pennsylvania. Logan was a scholar and *savant* of a very high order, founder of the Loganian Library at Philadelphia, and author of several scientific papers and treatises, some of which, in Latin, were published at Leyden. Among others with whom Logan corresponded was Thomas Story, whose house in Philadelphia Logan rented after Story's return to England. Some of the letters are printed in "Logan's Life, by Armistead," and exhibit him in a very pleasant light, sending presents to Logan's daughters, and doing such-like little friendly offices. In 1736, Chief-Justice Logan delivered to the Grand Inquest, at a Court of Oyer and Terminer and General Gaol Delivery, held for the city and county of Philadelphia, an elaborate charge, intended as a confutation of Hobbes, and based on the axiom, "That man was primarily, in his nature, formed for society;" a thesis from which Logan argued up to the necessity of penal laws and their administrative machinery. Of this charge, Logan sent a copy to Thomas Story, and, from Story's answer in reply, we glean that he held, on scientific points, opinions far in advance of his day, and abreast of those put forward by professors and philosophers now living, who would be astonished to think that, in 1736, any one, much less a Quaker preacher, held such views. Story's theory was, that "the Creator of all things never made anything dead, in its first procedure from him, but living,"—or, as he puts it, "that all inert matter was generally animated, consisting of innumerable animalculæ and farinæ *before the worlds were made of it.*" Some papers which Story wrote upon this subject appear to be lost, and so his arguments in support of his proposition are unknown. They appear to have taken some such line of reasoning as this: all seeds of animals, (animalculæ,) and all seeds of vegetables, (farinæ,) exist in the bodies of their parents (animal or vegetable,) grow to perfection, and decay, returning to earth, from whence they were borrowed and used for a time, "so that there is a perpetual revolution of all things, but no proper annihilation of any, save only of germ, but not of substance." As, therefore such never die, Story argues, they must have had life before God made the world of them, and that God endowed with life everything that he did create. This is not unlike a glimmering of Professor Huxley's theory of "protoplasms." In another epistle, Story intimates his belief in doctrines, at which, even now, many people would be astonished, not to say shocked. He had been to Scarborough, and, from a geological study of the cliffs there, he was confirmed in an opinion, "that the earth is of much older date, as to the beginning of it, than the time assigned in the Holy Scriptures, as commonly understood, which is suited to the common capacities of human kind, as to six days' progressive work, by which I understand certain long and competent periods of time, and not natural days, the time of the commencement and finishing of all those great works being undiscoverable by the mind of man, and hid in that short period, 'In the beginning God created the heavens and the earth.'" And then the author goes on to set forth "the further modifications of the terraqueous globe, and, I conjecture, very long after it had its being with the rest of the worlds." So far as this passage goes, Story might have been a pupil of Sir Charles Lyell himself. From other passages, also, we find that he believed in a plurality of worlds. It is curious that, in his own journal, he hints at none of these opinions. They are hardly such as the Society of Friends would have then approved of. During the latter part of Story's life, he was attacked by some members of the Society, and very much harassed, at the yearly meetings in London. We have also seen in print, a letter, written after his death, assuring Friends that Story died in unity with the Society. May not his opinions have brought him into some discredit with the more orthodox of the Society?

We have endeavoured to give a slight sketch of one who is deserving, if ever man was, to be ranked among the highest and best of our Cumberland worthies. Thomas Story was no vulgar religious ranter; he was a man of good position, of great learning, and, at one time, a conveyancing counsel in large practice. He gave up all his prospects in life because he considered it his duty to embrace the tenets of the Society of Friends; and he spent the best part of his life in ministering in Friends' meetings, not only in Great Britain and Ireland, but in America, where he spent many years of his life, and on the Continent.

Story himself is an authority for spelling his native place as we have done,—Justice Town, and not Justus Town, as it is generally spelt now-a-days.

Two sermons by Thomas Story, preached by him at York, in 1738, on Salvation by Christ, and on Silent Waiting, Silent Teaching, and Silent

Worship, have recently been printed and published, by Kitto, London, and Hudson Scott and Sons, Carlisle, from the original edition of 1738, which Story himself revised. In his journal, he thus alludes to these sermons:—

"I continued some time in these parts, and was again at the Quarterly Meeting at York, the business whereof was conducted in the peaceable wisdom of the Son of God; many great and important truths were delivered in the meetings, by several brethren, in the demonstration and authority of the Holy Spirit. Here a person took down some of my testimonies, in short-hand, as he had done before at some other times; this is seldom truly done, for though the form of the speech may be, by this means, and help of the memory of the writer, nearly preserved, yet the missing or altering of a word in some sentences, may greatly alter and wrong the sense; and it is certain, that no letters, words, or speech can represent the Divine virtue, power, and energy, in which the doctrines of the truth are delivered, by those who are sent of God, for they speak with wisdom and authority, in, and from Him."

SAMUEL BOWNAS.

SAMUEL BOWNAS, of Great Strickland, was born in Westmorland, within the compass of Great Strickland Monthly Meeting, in the year 1676. His father, a cordwainer, or shoemaker, who had suffered, in the days of Charles II., both in person and property, for his adhesion to the Society of Friends, died within a month after Samuel's birth, leaving his widow a subsistence of £4 10s. a-year, and a dwelling-house, on which to support herself and two children. Samuel Bownas thus got little education, for he was taken from school when ten years old, and set to keep sheep. He could do little more than read the Scriptures in his mother tongue. At the age of thirteen, he was put to learn the trade of a blacksmith, with an uncle, who used him very unkindly; but he was afterwards bound apprentice to Samuel Parat, near Sedburgh, who provided his apprentice with both work and meat enough. Samuel, at this time, took but little heed of religious matters. He used to frequent meetings of the Society, but generally slept during them, and thus acquired little benefit, except that of being kept out of bad company. He also acquired the reputation of a wit in conversation. One "First Day," when Samuel was at meeting, "a young woman, named Ann Wilson, was there and preached. She was very zealous, and, fixing my eye upon her, she with a great zeal pointed her finger at me, uttering these words, with much power, 'A traditional Quaker, thou comest to meeting as thou went from it the last time, and goes from it as thou came to it, but art no better for thy coming. What wilt thou do in the end?'" This address wrought a change in Bownas. The lessons which his mother had, in very early childhood, instilled into his mind, recurred to him, and also the recollection of seeing her "greeting" over Friends who had been carried off to Appleby Gaol. From a traditional Quaker, he became a zealous one, with a burning desire to speak at the meetings, which the suddenness of his conversion compelled him to restrain. He did, however, burst out, about four weeks after his conversion, with a short testimony or address to the meeting he was attending. This happened on Christmas Day, 1696, which fell on a Sunday. His apprenticeship had then about three years to run, and during the rest of it he, as he tells us, "said very little." When his apprenticeship was over, in his 21st year, he went a journey, with Isaac Alexander, through Yorkshire, Lancashire, Cumberland, and Scotland. They travelled on foot, and Bownas's mind became "darkened," so that he groaned aloud, which his companion misunderstood, thinking it was produced by excessive fatigue. On his return, Bownas's worldly wealth was reduced to three-halfpence; but he picked up some money by harvesting, and contrived to purchase a horse, on which he started, with Alexander, for the West of England. They did not get very far before Bownas "was shut up, and had no satisfaction at all in going farther with him." They parted, and Bownas wandered on by himself, in great distress of mind, preaching at various places, and receiving much kindness from older and eminent preachers. At times, he felt minded to abscond, sell his horse, get to some port in Ireland, and work as a blacksmith; at others, to make away with himself. Neither of these plans could he effect, for the Society, either suspecting his troubles, or from caution, always provided him with a guide from place to place. The kindness and advice of such Friends as Camm, Dickenson, Fearon, Boustead, and others, appears to have been of great use to him. In particular, they persuaded him to suppress a call he felt to go to London and proclaim a great mortality which was to fall upon the Friends as a punishment. Alexander had already declared this at Bristol, but the Elders of the Society there sent him home at once. Bownas took advice before he said anything about it, and was told to wait.

Bownas returned home, and, as his linen and woollen clothes were both in need of renewal, he returned to the smithy, and worked hard all the summer, until he saved some cash, preparatory to starting on another tour to the West of England. On this tour, he was at some places taken for "a Cheat (viz., a Jesuit in disguise)." At others, people would have it that he was a disfrocked minister. He also got acquainted with a Friend who afterwards became his wife, whose name he nowhere informs us of. He proposed to the lady and her parents, but told them that he had a call first to visit America. To this they consented; but a wealthy uncle interfered, and insisted that no engagement should be entered into; that Bownas should, by writing, bind himself; but that the lady should not be bound at all. She, however, objected to this, and they parted without an engagement. Returning again to the North, Bownas went to mowing during the harvest. While in the North, he went to a meeting at Goose Green, between Kendal and Milnthorpe, where John Boustead and Peter Fearon attended. Out of this meeting grew a controversy between Bownas and the schoolmaster of Beathams, (this name is doubtful; it is illegible in the copy of Bownas's journal before us,) about Infant Baptism. A place and time were fixed for a public argument. The schoolmaster brought his parish priest to back him; while Bownas brought John Jopson, schoolmaster, of Kendal, to help him by references to the Greek and Latin Testaments, if necessary. The vehemence and hotness of the parson, an old man, "having a comely personage and fine white locks," broke up the meeting, without any result, except that his schoolmaster became a Friend.

In August, 1701, Bownas and one Isaac Thompson went a journey into Scotland. At Dumfries, they met, in their inn, James Dickenson and some other Friends. After refreshment, Dickenson said, "Lads, I find a concern to go into the street; will you go with me?" Friends were seldom seen there; a crowd soon collected, who heard Dickenson preach with attention, though some were rude. Bownas proceeded, by Hamilton, Glasgow (where the people were rude, but not so uncivil as in former days), Inverary, Aberdeen, Ury, Edinburgh, and Kelso, to Jedburgh, where he was treated to "Jeddart law." He was not hung first, and tried afterwards, but he was put into the Tolbooth for preaching, before he had begun to preach. Bownas hoped to preach from the Tolbooth windows, as two Westmorland Friends, Isaac Thompson and Thomas Braithwaite, had done the week before. The provost, however, boarded the window grates up. Next day some powerful country gentleman interfered, and compelled the provost to release Bownas and his companions. This was on market-day, and Bownas preached from the Market Cross to about five thousand people,—the streets, and the house balconies and windows being crammed. The town officers, after he had concluded, dragged him to the Tolbooth door. The guard-chamber was close by, and one of the sentinels, apparently an Englishman, if not a Westmorland man, interfered, clubbed his musket, and insisted that Bownas should first be taken before the provost for examination. This the officers declined to do. Bownas got free, and preached from the Tolbooth steps. As Bownas retired to his inn, he was treated with great respect, a lane made for him, the people crying, "Well done! you have dung (beaten) them, sir." At his inn several gentlemen assembled, and much discourse took place about religion; finally, Bownas, at their request, related the story of his life, and how he came to be a preacher. From Jedburgh, he proceeded home, by Solport and Carlisle.

In October, 1701, Bownas went up to London to embark for America. He had, on account of the French war, to wait until March, 1702, before he could get a ship. He himself thought little of the danger of being captured by the French; but, on his arrival at Philadelphia, he heard that Thomas Story, of Justice Town, had been taken by a French privateer, and carried into Martinique.

When Bownas arrived in America, he received a note from George Keith, the famous apostate Friend:—

"*To the Preacher lately arrived from England.*

"Sir,—I intend to give notice, after sermon, that you and myself are to dispute to-morrow, and would have you give notice thereof accordingly."

Bownas's reply was as follows:—

"George Keith,—I have received thine; and think myself no way obliged to take any notice of one that hath been so very mutable in his pretences to religion. Besides, as thou hast long since been disowned, after due admonition given thee by our Yearly Meetings in London, for thy quarrelsome and irregular practices, thou art not worthy of my notice, being no more to me than a heathen man and a publican — Is the needful from

"SAMUEL BOWNAS."

Near Chester, in Maryland, Bownas visited a Society of communists, called Labadies, about one hundred in number, men, women, and children, who, in their practices, resembled some of the modern strange Societies which have sprung up in America. Bownas records that this Society was afterwards dispersed. Journeying on to Philadelphia, Bownas was taken ill with ague, and laid up for many weeks. On recovering, he met George Keith at a dinner, whereat great attempts were made to entangle Bownas in his talk, which he skilfully avoided. Keith's friends next attended Bownas's meetings, took notes of his doctrines, and filed depositions charging him with defaming the Church of England. On these depositions, Bownas was committed for trial, and sent to gaol, as he refused to give bail. After some time, the Assizes were opened by Chief-Justice Bridges and Justice Miller, with great pomp, preceded by trumpets and music. The grand jury ignored the bills against Bownas, and stuck to their decision, though much bullied and abused by Bridges, who sent Bownas back to gaol, threatening to send him to England chained to the deck of a man-of-war. On Bownas's return to prison, he was visited by Thomas Hicks, late Chief-Justice of the province, who blamed Lord Cornbury, the Governor, for the illegality to which Bownas had been subjected, and bid him be of good cheer, for Lord Cornbury and Bridges dare not send him to England, nor could they get a jury to find a true bill.

Bownas was confined in a small log house; and, by the help of a Scotchman, Charles Williams, he learnt how to make shoes, and supported himself by that, earning fifteen shillings a-week. The Friends hardly liked this, for they wished to support him by contributions.

Bownas had a most remarkable visitor in his captivity,—namely, an Indian King, whose words should, surely, shame all persecutors. He inquired if Bownas was a Christian, and hearing he was, asked if his keepers were Christians, and was astonished to hear that they were so too. In the course of a most remarkable conversation, the Indian inquired closely into the differences of religious opinions which had led to Bownas being a prisoner, and, on learning that they consisted of questions about the sprinkling of water at baptism, the celebration of the Lord's Supper, the illegality of war, and of uncovering before men, was astonished, observing that "the Mang Manettay (or Indian God) look'd at the heart how it was devoted, and not at these childish things."

In 1703, a second grand jury again ignored the bills against Bownas, and the Judge (Bridges was dead) ordered him to be set free on paying his fees. By proclamation, however, Bownas was discharged without that; and a sort of triumph was celebrated over his release, after nearly a year's confinement. Bownas now travelled from place to place. He writes, that in some places, during worship, and various classes assembling, fire arms were ranged against the meeting-house wall, in case of Indian attacks.

In 1706, Bownas returned to England, and found "his friend" waiting for him through six years' absence. They were soon married,—a great number of "publick Friends" being present on the occasion. He now settled at Lymington, among his wife's friends, and went into business as a maltster. After being there for three years, he got into hot water about tithes, and was pulled up before Justice Philips, who was rough and uncourteous, and Justice Harben, who was mild and easy, even offering to pay the arrears out of his own pocket. Bownas would not allow this; and was, at last, arrested and sent to gaol. After ten days' confinement, the parson, who claimed the tithes, which were thirteen years in arrear, procured his release, but instituted a suit in the Exchequer. A relation of Bownas, a large grazier, then came and borrowed ten pounds from Mrs. Bownas, and when he had got it, flung down the parson's receipt for his tithes, and informed her that he had compromised all demands for that sum, and that he would rather have paid it himself than seen Bownas and his wife ruined by the Exchequer suit. Bownas was extremely angry at this friendly trick, but could not help himself. He had a long correspondence with the parson, William Ray by name, on the legality of tithes. Ray put his case in a manner that is both kind and lawyer-like.

In 1717, Bownas visited Cornwall. In 1719, his wife died. The only thing that troubled her on her deathbed was, that she had been deceived about the parson's tithe.

Bownas now disposed of his business, and let

his estate. He travelled to Cumberland, and visited meetings there. At Cockermouth, he fell in with the Ranters, Job Pearson and his brother, whom we have mentioned in our account of Thomas Story. The Pearsons found congenial employment in fighting in an alehouse, and so engaged themselves too much to come and interrupt Bownas. In 1722, he married, a second time, a widow named Nichols. They went to London together, and returned to Lymington in a coach, —the first and only mention we find of one in the books we have been consulting in writing these memoirs; on foot, or more commonly on horseback, was then the universal mode of travelling.

In 1726, Bownas paid a second visit to America, much to his wife's misliking. His son-in-law, Josiah Nickleson, went with him. There he remained for eighteen months. His voyage back was attended with great dangers. A hurricane dismasted the vessel, and swept overboard most of the stock of water and live provisions, reducing the crew to short commons. The last part of their voyage was very tedious; now they sighted the Lizard, now the Eddystone, looking in the distance like the mast of a ship; and each time were blown out to sea again. At last they got into Plymouth, and Bownas took horse and went to his own house.

There is little more to note in Bownas's life. His second wife died in 1746. He continued to travel, frequently visiting Cumberland, and going to Ireland by Whitehaven or Workington, and attending meetings at Cockermouth, Pardsay, Whitehaven, Allonby, Broughton, Holme Cultram, Wigton, Moorhouse, Carlisle, Caldbeck, Penrith, and other places. He mentions that the three largest Quarterly Meetings of any in England were those of Cumberland, Westmorland, and Lancashire. This was in 1747. His journal ceases in 1749, and he died in 1753, prior to which his eyesight had failed, and his hands became shaky. He was aged seventy-seven.

He was a man of grave deportment; tall, comely, and manly in appearance; with a clear, strong, and distinct voice.

His journal was published in 1756.

THE BEWLEYS.

Of this name, several are celebrated in the early annals of the Society of Friends. GEORGE BEWLEY, of Ivegill; GEORGE BEWLEY, of Hesketh; GEORGE BEWLEY, of Woodhall, (these two latter are probably one and the same); MUNGO BEWLEY, of Carlisle; and "Old THOMAS BEWLEY, of Cumberland," all appear to have been preachers, and sufferers for their faith. Mungo Bewley was one of the companions of John Banks, of Brigham, in his imprisonment at Carlisle. Old Thomas Bewley entertained George Fox on several occasions. We can find little information as to any of the Bewleys, except George Bewley, of Ivegill.

This George Bewley was born in 1684, and began to attend meetings of Friends when only seven years old. About the age of twelve or thirteen, religious matters occupied his mind very much, and, in particular, he was much distressed at people sleeping during religious services. When about seventeen years old, some Friends from Ireland visited Cumberland, and took George Bewley back to Ireland with them, where he was apprenticed to a linen-draper. In the year 1702, George Bewley, of Ivegill, was (according to a broadsheet of that date, preserved in the valuable collection of the Honourable Society of Lincoln's Inn,) prosecuted by Sir Edward Hasell, of Dalemain, for non-payment of tithes. In that year, Sir Edward, according to the broadsheet, seized, under a writ, cattle belonging to Bewley to the value of £39, to cover a claim amounting to only £3 10s. In the following year he seized, to cover the same claim, cattle to the value of £23 10s. This George Bewley, of Ivegill, must have been father of the George Bewley, who was born in 1684, and who went to Ireland. There he settled altogether, though at intervals he visited Cumberland, married one Blessing Fennell, and died there in 1749. This George was cousin to Mungo Bewley, of Carlisle, and many of his descendants are now living at Dublin, esteemed members of the Society.

In Fox's journal, it is told that George Bewley and Joseph Hellen tried to convince one Blanch Pope, "a Ranting woman." She was too much for them, for she asked, "Who made the Devil, did God?" This question, as Fox records, puzzled the two so much as to shake their faith. Hellen actually left the Society; but Bewley, under Fox's guidance, was confirmed.

JOHN AND THOMAS STUBBS.

JOHN STUBBS was a soldier in the garrison of Carlisle, and was convinced by George Fox, while Fox was in prison at that place. He was discharged from the army because he refused, from objections to swearing at all, to take the oath of allegiance to Cromwell. He was skilled in the Latin, Greek, Hebrew, and Oriental languages; and, after his convincement, travelled to Rome, and into the dominions of the Grand Turk. While on his travels, the hand of Sir Daniel Fleming appears to have fallen heavily on Stubbs's wife and children, but this is all we know of him.

THOMAS STUBBS, of Dean, was, with one Peter Head, sent to Carlisle Gaol, in 1654, at the instance of Launcelot Fletcher. Stubbs and Head were brought before Justice Thomas Cholmeley and Justice William Brisco, who signed a *mittimus* for their committal to gaol, and then an order for their liberation. They were detained for their fees. The Clerk of the Peace demanded 4s. 8d. a-piece, the Sheriff 6s. 8d., and the gaoler 10s. These demands they declined to pay, and insisted on seeing a copy of the *mittimus* under which they were sent to prison, as, they contended, it was bad in law. This was refused them; and they appealed to the Mayor of Carlisle, who thereon ordered them to be deprived of pen and ink. Charles Howard, afterwards the first Earl of Carlisle, is recorded as having borne testimony for them; but the Sheriff, Wilfred Lawson, is mentioned as being very hot against them. Of the termination of their imprisonment we find no mention. The record from which we quote, an Appeal by Stubbs and Head against the injustice of their imprisonment, makes careful note of the fact that Justice Cholmely died within a short time after signing the *mittimus* under which Stubbs and Head were committed; while of Briscoe it says, "God rebuked him,"—an allusion, we fancy, to a story we have already told.

BARNARD BARTON.

BARNARD BARTON, of High Head, was also a member of the Society of Friends, and a descendant of a family whose pedigree, for many generations back, may be found in the books of Dalston Church. He was a claimant to be considered the inventor of the spinning-jenny. We have little information about him, except the following note, written by Miss Jane Christian Blamire, sister of the late M.P. for Cumberland, and kindly furnished to us by a friend :—

"In this book my beloved mother was much pleased and interested on the evening of the 14th March, 1837, sitting up later than her usual [time,] and talking of the worth and great ability of old Barny Barton, of High Head, the ancestor of the poet, and inventor of the spinning-jenny. On his invention Arkwright improved, and established in his works at Matlock, in Derbyshire, after their having been destroyed in different places, and which have now attained such wonderful perfection.

"In remembrance of Mrs. Blamire, who departed this life, March 15, 1837."

[*Written on the fly-leaf at the commencement of "The Reliquery: by Bernard and Lucy Barton."*]

Barny Barton was buried in the graveyard of St. Cuthbert's Church, Carlisle. On his tomb is the following legend :—

"Erected to the Memory of Barnard Barton, who died January 6th, 1773, aged 45 years. Also of Mary, his Wife, who died May 20th, 1786, aged 54 years. Also of Five of their Children, viz., George, William, Abraham, Henry, and Barnard, who died in their infancy.

"Repaired and re-erected by Bernard and John Barton, grandsons of the first-named deceased, 1846."

[*Headstone in St. Cuthbert's Churchyard, Carlisle.*]

MISCELLANEOUS FRIENDS.

Although we have gone through most of the more eminent local preachers and members of the Society of Friends, yet we have by no means exhausted the list. Plenty of other names can be found, of preachers well known and honoured in their day by the Society of Friends. There is a JONATHAN BURNYEAT, son of John Burnyeat, mentioned by James Dickenson in his journal, travelling with him at various times, as a minister in his boyhood. At the age of thirteen years, he is spoken of by James Dickenson as "deeply opened into the mysteries of God's kingdom, and grew in his gift, so as to give counsel to young and old. He was very zealous against deceit and wickedness, both in professor and profane, and often reproved such." He died at Graythwaite, near Crabtree-beck, in Cumberland, 1709, in the 23rd year of his age. There are also JOHN and ALICE ALDERSON, of Ravenstonedale, both ministers. ALICE preached in America, Scotland, and Ireland, and died, aged eighty-eight, in 1766, at Ravenstonedale. ELIZABETH BRAITHWAITE, of Kendal, who died in prison there, aged seventeen, in 1684. THOMAS CARLETON, an author and a poet; JOSEPH GILL, of Skelton; EDWARD GAY, of Appleby; BENJAMIN HOLMES, of Kendal, a most voluminous writer, whose works have been translated into Dutch, Latin, and French; THOMAS HOLMES, the earliest missionary to the Welsh; JOHN SALKELD, of Cumberland, who gained great celebrity in America; JOHN BECK, of Dockra; THOMAS LAITHES, of Dailehead; JOHN STEEL; THOMAS SCOTT, of Newbiggen; JOSEPH BUNTING, of Allonby; THOMAS WILKINSON, of Beckfoot; THOMAS DREWERY, of Bolton; JOHN THOMPSON, of Crook, near Kendal; WILLIAM and SARAH DIXON, of Waterend, near Loweswater; GEORGE ROOKE, of Bolton; WILLIAM WILLIAMSON, of Windermere; HUGH TICKELL, of Portinscale; WILLIAM CARTER, of Cumberland,—all might be added to the list of worthies we have gone through in these papers. Of all these, short accounts are to be found in now forgotten tracts, in the libraries belonging to various Meetings of the Society of Friends.

Of apostate Friends, the two counties have produced one or two, such as JAMES HOSKINS, of Cumberland, who settled in London, and embittered the latter days of Thomas Story, of Justice Town, by writing abusive pamphlets against him; and JOHN GILPIN, of Kendal, who wrote "The Quaker Shaken; or, A Firebrand snatch'd out of the Fire: Being a briefe Relation of God's wonderful Mercie extended to John Gilpin, of Kendale, in Westmorland, who, as will appear by the Sequel, was not only deluded, but possessed by the Devil."

The PEARSONS, of Wigton, and the annoyances they inflicted on the Society, have more than once been referred to in the course of these papers. JOHN SENHOUSE, of Wigton, in 1718, lashed them in a book, which he called "Outrageous Apostates Exposed; or, A Relation of the monstrous Outrages, Errors, and Blasphemies committed by Isaac Pearson and his impious Associates, upon several occasions, but more especially in Meetings held for the Performance of Divine Service and Worship of Almighty God, by the People called Quakers, in the County of Cumberland."

The voluminous literature of the Society of Friends is but little known; and yet it presents a perfect mine of information as to the manners and customs of England. Had Lord Macaulay been acquainted with it, we feel certain he would have much modified the character he gives of George Fox in his History. For instance, strange as it may appear to us, it was usual, in the times of the Commonwealth, for the parish church to be used, out of the regular service hours, by ministers of all sorts of denominations; and the priests were ready enough, in many cases, to hold discussions there with preachers not of their own persuasion. Thus the proceedings of Fox and his disciples in "steeple-houses" were far from being as outrageous then, as they would now be considered.

In these papers, it has been no part of the writer's plan to discuss the distinguishing religious principles of the early Friends; but, rather, to note remarkable historical facts and features of the times, connected with the two counties of Cumberland and Westmorland, and relating to the early Friends, and the struggle they had to maintain for many years against heavy fines and long imprisonments, in defence of that large measure of religious freedom that we all now inherit as a *purchased* possession. An early Friend, John Scott, of Brownrigg, near Caldbeck, great grandfather of a gentleman now well known in Carlisle, placed over the door of Brownrigg Hall, (built by him in 1694,) the following verse, still distinct and legible, which illustrates the most distinguishing doctrine of the Society of Friends:—

> "GRACE brings salvation by an inward light,
> Works reformation in a pious sight:
> Then listen well unto Christ's voice within,
> And tender that which keeps us out of sin."

APPENDIX.

APPENDIX.

As a striking record of the penalties and sufferings inflicted on the early Quakers for nonconformity to ecclesiastical law, and in defence of liberty of conscience towards God, we append the following account, taken from "Besse's Sufferings," volume I., which are thus entitled, and published in two thick folio volumes: "A Collection of the Sufferings of the People called Quakers, for the Testimony of a Good Conscience, from the Time of their being first distinguished by that Name, in the year 1650, to the Time of the *Act of Toleration*, granted to Protestant Dissenters in the First Year of the Reign of King William the Third and Queen Mary, in the Year 1689. Taken from Authentic Records and other Authentic Accounts, by Joseph Besse":—

CUMBERLAND.

Anno 1653.

George Fox, for Preaching the Truth in the great Worship-house at *Carlisle*, after the Priest had ended his Sermon, and for witnessing a good Confession before the Magistrates and People there, was imprisoned seven Weeks, sometimes among Thieves and Murderers.

Robert Withers, for asking the Priest of *Aketon* a religious Question after Sermon, was imprisoned at *Carlisle* one Month; as was *George Bewly* for accompanying him. *Robert Huntington*, for preaching at *Carlisle*, was imprisoned *three Months*, and *James Noble*, for the same cause, *nine Weeks*.

Robert Withers, *Thomas Rawlinson*, *John Stubbs*, and *Thomas Gwin*, for declaring against false Worship at the Steeple-house in *Coldbeck*, were inhumanly treated by the rude People, one of them being knocked down, and much of their Blood spilled on the Place.

John Martin, for testifying against the Priest of *Kirkbride*, whom he met in the Fields, and calling him by his proper Name, *viz. an Hireling*, was committed to Prison.

ANNO 1654.

Thomas Stubbs was concerned to go into the Steeple-house at *Deane*, where, when the Priest had done, he said, *Thou daubest the People up with untempered Mortar;* whereupon the Priest bid his Hearers *fight for the Gospel;* they fell violently upon *Stubbs* and some of his friends, tore their Clothes, and beat them cruelly. The Priest's Son in particular sorely bruised the face of *Richard Richardson*. After which two Justices sent *Stubbs* to Prison, but conscious of the wrong they did him, writ his *Mittimus* and *Discharge* both on one Paper; this furnished the Gaoler with a Claim for Fees, under Pretence of which he kept him fourteen Weeks in Prison.

Peter Head, for testifying to the Truth, in the same Place, was imprisoned fourteen Weeks in a close Room among Felons in the Heat of Summer; and *John Head*, for delivering some Queries to the Priest of *Deane* at his own House, was imprisoned fourteen Weeks. *John Slee*, for reproving a Priest at *Grisdale*, was kept a close Prisoner among Felons two Months. Also *Katharine Fell*, for asking a Priest, *Whether he did witness what he spake to the People*, was kept in Prison nineteen Weeks, having a young Child sucking at her Breast.

Thomas Bewley and *Hugh Stamper*, standing at the Sessions in *Carlisle* with their Hats on, were by the Justices committed to Prison without any legal Cause assigned. After a Month's Confinement they were discharged without paying Fees: But *Hugh Stamper* was afterward arrested for Fees, and again imprisoned and detained there one and twenty Weeks.

ANNO 1655.

Matthew Carpe and *Anthony Fell* were imprisoned for appearing at Sessions with their Hats on, and detained three Weeks.

Matthew Robinson and *John Dixon*, for refusing to pay Tithes, were imprisoned at *Carlisle*, and afterward obliged to appear personally at *London*, above two Hundred and fifty Miles from their Habitations, to their great Expence and Trouble.

John Peacock and *John Stricket*, Constables, refusing to

execute a Warrant of Distress for Tithes, were fined 1*l.* 6*s.* 8*d.*, and for Non-payment committed to Prison.

Dorothy Waugh, for Preaching in the Streets of *Carlisle*, and *Anne Robinson*, who accompanied her, were by the Mayor sent to Prison, and some Time after were led through the Street with each an Iron Instrument of Torture, called a Bridle, on their Heads, to prevent their speaking to the People; having been so exposed to the Scorn and Derision of the Rabble, they were turned out of the City.

John Westray and *Thomas Scott* were cruelly beaten by the rude People, for testifying against the doctrine of the Preacher at *Seck-Murder* Chapel.

ANNO 1657.

The following Persons were imprisoned at *Carlisle* for reproving the Priests at several Times and Places, *viz. John Grave* twenty-two Weeks, *George Bewley* fourteen Weeks, *John Burnyeat* twenty-three Weeks. *Matthew Robinson* twenty-nine Weeks, *Anthony Tickle* twenty-seven Weeks, and *George Wilson*.

ANNO 1660.

In this and the several foregoing Years had been taken from Persons in this County by Distress, for 156*l.* 8*s.* 7*d.* demanded for Tithes, Goods worth 515*l.* 1*s.* 3*d.* And for Demands of 3*l.* 12*s.* 3*d.* for Steeple-house Rates and Clerk's Wages, Goods to the Value of 11*l.* 13*s.* 10*d.*

In this Year also *Francis Hayton* and *William Rowland* were imprisoned for Tithes thirty-two Weeks.

John Robinson, for refusing to take an Oath at *Carlisle* Assizes, was fined 40*s.*, and had Goods taken from him to that Value.

In the same Year *Thomas Stordy* was imprisoned nine Weeks for refusing to take the Oath of Allegiance; and for the same Cause *James Adamson* was kept close Prisoner several Weeks, during which Time, his Father, of the same Name, coming to visit him, was way-laid in his Return home, and by a Justice of the Peace sent back to Prison for refusing to swear. For the same Cause also *Elizabeth Heath*, *Anne Bewley*, *Elizabeth Jackson*, *Elizabeth Hazard*, *William Oglethorp*, *Anne* his Wife, *Isabel Oglethorp*, and *Elizabeth Watson*, suffered twenty-two Weeks' Imprisonment; Also *Thomas Summers*, *William Summers*, *Humphry*

Twiddale, and *Thomas Story*, were imprisoned fourteen Weeks, and * *William Lowthwait* one and thirty Weeks; *Thomas Watson*, *Richard Ribton*, *Christopher Manser*, *Richard Banks*, and *Thomas Leathes*, nine Days; *John Matthew*, of *Brough*, several Weeks; and *Robert Huntington*, *John Robinson*, *Robert Matthew*, and *Margaret Martin*, twenty-two Weeks, which last four were taken up in *Carlisle* Market, being there about their lawful Occasions, and sent to Gaol by the Mayor for refusing the Oath.

ANNO 1661.

John Nicholson, *Thomas Mark*, and *John Peacock*, on an attachment out of the *Exchequer*, were committed to *Carlisle* Gaol in the Month called *April* this Year, and detained there about three Years.

In this Year also *George Biglands* and *John Dobinson* suffered eight Weeks' Imprisonment for refusing to Swear; and for the same Cause *Christoper Manser* had a Cow taken from him worth 2*l*. 4*s*., and *Christopher Birkett* a Cow worth 3*l*.

ANNO 1662.

In this Year *Adam Robinson*, *William Bond*, and *John Richardson*, suffered about seven Months' Imprisonment, having been arrested for Tithes at the Suit of *Francis Howard*, of *Corby*, a *Papist*, who afterward at the Assizes obtained Judgment against them for treble Damages, upon which were taken from

		l.	*s.*	*d.*		*l.*	*s.*	*d.*
Adam Robinson,	for a Demand of	1	5	0	four Beasts worth	28	0	0
William Bond,	for a Demand of	0	7	0	a Mare and Steer	3	15	0
John Richardson,	for a Demand of	1	12	0	Cattle worth	7	10	0
	For Demands of	3	4	0	Goods worth	39	5	0

In this Year also, for refusing to Swear at the Mannour Courts, were taken from

		l.	*s.*	*d.*		*l.*	*s.*	*d.*
Richard Thompson,	for a Fine of	3	6	8	a Cow worth	3	0	0
Francis Hayton,	for a Fine of	0	3	4	Goods worth	0	8	0
Thomas Hunter,	for a Fine of	3	6	8	Kine worth	6	0	0
	For Fines of	6	16	8	Goods worth	9	8	0

* *W. Lowthwait* had offended a Neighbouring Justice's Servant by reproving him for profane Swearing; whereupon the Justice, to revenge his Man's Quarrel, tendered *William* the Oath, and sent him to Prison.

Thomas Stordy, being at *Carlisle* Assizes, went to visit some of his Friends there in Prison, but was illegally detained by the Gaoler, and the next Day, he, with *Stephen Pearson*, then a Prisoner, was had to the Sessions-house, where the Oath of Allegiance was tendered them, which they refusing, were sent back to Gaol among the Felons: Next Day they were indicted on the Statute of 3 K. *James*, found *guilty*, and had Sentence of *Premunire* passed upon them; by which they were adjudged *to forfeit all their Lands, Goods, and Chattels, to be out of the King's Protection, and to suffer Imprisonment for Life.* Soon after the Sheriff seized their Cattle, Corn, and other Goods, and proclaimed a publick Sale of them, at which they were sold far beneath the Value, in regard very few cared to buy them. However, they were at length disposed of and carried away, without any Regard to the Prisoners or their Families, nor would the Sheriff, though earnestly desired, allow any thing to the poor Labourers, who had been employed in gathering in the Corn, and whom the Prisoners, thus plundered, were unable to pay. Under this hard Sentence *Thomas Stordy* and *Stephen Pearson* continued close Prisoners several Years, enduring their great Sufferings with exemplary Patience and Constancy, being supported by the Testimony of a good Conscience in their Obedience to the Precept of Christ, *Swear not at all.*

John Grave, of *Torpenhow*, *Thomas Watson*, of *Cockermouth*, and *John Robinson*, of *Brigham*, taken out of their own Houses by Soldiers, and carried to the Governor of *Carlisle*, were by him imprisoned, in the Depth of Winter, in a cold Place over one of the City Gates, where they were denied the Visits of their Friends, and had their Food frequently kept from them, nor were they permitted to go out to ease themselves: After about ten Days' Confinement there, the Oath was tendered them at a Meeting of the Justices, and they were removed to the County Gaol, where they lay thirty-five Weeks. In the same year *John Slee* had two Steers, worth 9*l.*, taken from him for a Fine of 5*l.* for being at a Meeting; and on the 7th of the Month called *August*, *Richard Ribton*, *William Ribton*, and *Thomas Ashley*, of *Great Broughton*, *Christopher Shepherd* and *John Shepherd*, of *Ribton*, *Christopher Palmer* and *William Hall*, of *Little-Broughton*, *John Parker*, of *Pop-Castle*, and *Launcelot Wilson*, of *Tallontire*, were summoned before the Justices on an Information against them for Meeting, and sent to Prison till the Assizes, when they were indicted, and having pleaded *not guilty*, were recommitted till another Assizes, before which *Lancelot Wilson* died in the Prison, being a weakly Man, and unable to sustain the Hardship of his Confinement. At the following Assizes the rest of them were discharged. In this year, also, *George Fletcher*, a Justice of the Peace, signalized himself by a violent Procedure at a Meeting at *Howhill*, in *Sowerby* Parish, into which he, with a Retinue armed with Swords and Pistols, rushed in after an hostile Manner, and finding a Person on his Knees, the Justice struck him over the Head, and when he contined Praying, ordered him to be pulled down backward, and then caused him, together with *John Slee*, *George Bewley*, *Mungo Bewley*, *Anthony Fell*, *John Banks*, and others of the Assembly, to be dragged down the Hill in a violent and cruel Manner, and afterward sent them to *Carlisle* Gaol. At the next Sessions *John Slee* was fined 10*l.*, and the rest 5*l.* each, for which Fines were taken, from *John Slee*, three Kine, one Bull, and an Heifer, worth 13*l.* : from *George Bewley*, three Kine, werth 8*l.* ; and from *Mungo Bewley*, two Horses, worth 5*l.* 2*s.* 6*d.* At the Time of making these Distresses, *George Bewley* was remaining a Prisoner for the same Fine.

ANNO 1663.

Thomas Bewley, after frequent Seizures of his Goods for Tithes, was this Year, on an *Exchequer* Process, committed to Prison at *Carlisle*, where he lay near three Years. In this Year, also, Seizures were made on *James Stanton*, of *Westdale*, to the Value of 27*l.* and upwards, for a Demand of but 3*l.* for Tithes ; and on *Thomas Bewley* the younger, to the Value of 11*l.* for a Claim of 2*l.* 18*s.* for Tithes. And in the same Year, for Demands of 10*l.* 4*s.* 2½*d.* for Tithes, several others had Goods taken by Distress, to the Value of 30*l.* 1*s.* 11*d.* In this Year, also, suffered by Distress, for refusing te Swear, *Richard Fawcett*, 1*l.* 12*s.* *Philip Burnyeat*, 20*s.* ; *Henry Allason*, 50*s.* ; and *William Morrison*, 40*s.* Also, *Thomas Fell*, *John Fell*, *James Barnes*, and *John Tiffin*, were Sufferers by Distress on the same Account.

ANNO 1664.

Richard Fawcett, *John Gill*, *William Richardson*, and *John Fearon*, were prosecuted in the *Exchequer*, by *George Fletcher*, for

Tithes; the Claim he made from some of them was but 6*d.*, and from none of them above 1*s.*, for which Trifles some of them were obliged by the Prosecutor to appear several Times at *London*, two Hundred and fifty Miles from their Habitations: His Purpose being not so much to recover any Thing, as to perplex and harass the poor Men, who at length were imprisoned at *Carlisle* for refusing to Swear to the Answers they gave into Court. For the same Reason, also, *William Bowman*, *William Morrison*, and *John Fell*, were sent to Prison. In this Year, likewise, were imprisoned upon Writs *de Excommunicato capiendo*, after Prosecution in the Ecclesiastical Court for Tithes, *Hugh Tickell*, *Anthony Tickell*, *John Wilson*, *Anthony Wood*, *Christopher Scott*, *William Longstake*, *Thomas Stamper*, *Thomas Porter*, *John Pattinson*, *Thomas Fell*, *Thomas Carleton*, *John Gibson*, *William Adcock*, *Leonard Whitburne*, and *John Hetherington*.

In this and the foregoing Year, the generality of the *Quakers* in this County, Men, Women, and Children, were fined for *Nonconformity* to the established Worship, which Fines were rigorously exacted by Distresses made on Parents for their Children, Masters for their Servants, and even on such as, being themselves Conformists, had Servants or others in their Families who were not. The Sums of Money levied for this Cause in these two Years, amounted to 87*l.* 17*s.* 7d. We also find that within these last four Years, for Demands made for Steeple-house Rates and Clerks' Wages, amounting to 6*l.* 13*s.*, Distresses were made to the Value of 18*l.* 18*s.* 3*d.*

ANNO 1665.

Richard Banks, fined for being at a religious Meeting, had two Cows taken away which cost him 9*l.* 15*s.*

ANNO 1667.

In this Year a remarkable Case of the aforesaid *Richard Banks* occurring, we have extracted the same from a *Narrative* thereof written by himself, *viz.* :—

"In the Year 1667, *Lancelot Simpson* having purchased that "Estate which I farmed of him who was then my Landlord, in "the first Place excommunicated me, because I would not conform "to their Church, he being then, and now is, a Proctor, resolving "to make me submit, or else destroy me in the Outward, which "he hath very much laboured and endeavoured ever since: So, "pretending that all I had was too little to satisfy the Law, he "one Day, I being from Home, came, and one *Thomas Stamper* "with him, and nailed up the Garner-door, and went and turned "out all my Threshers, and nailed up the Barn-door, and after-"ward came in the Night Season, when the Snow lay thick on the "Earth, and we being all in Bed, got into the Stable and Byer, "and turned out all my Horses, and Cows with their young "Calves, by reason whereof some perished, and others hardly "escaped with Life: He also set his Men to pull down the Hedge "from about the Haystacks, and to keep his own Beasts at them, "and to put mine from them. Nay, farther, I had at that Time "nine Score Sheep, or thereabouts. He would suffer no Man to "buy them, but himself pretending a Title, and hindering others, "I was forced to take a third Penny after a long Contest, and the "Death of a third Part of them; by all which I deeply suffered. "Then I, seeing his Cruelty, was forced to seek another Farm, "which I got about twenty Miles off.— In a short Time after, "the said *Lancelot Simpson* arrested me with an *Excommunication* "Writ, and it being found to be out of Date, he was at that Time "prevented of his Purpose; and still his Cruelty lives against me "and my Wife, because he cannot make us bow, as is evident by "his many Fines against us, and now last of all by his apprehend-"ing both me and my Wife, and carrying us rigidly away from "our Children and Servants, I having at that very Time ten Men "at Work, these cruel Fellows would scarce let us speak to them. "So we being carried away Prisoners, and straitly lookt to, as "Thieves and Felons, in our Way to the Prison met with *Lancelot* "*Simpson*, and after some Discourse before many Witnesses, I "asked him, *If I owed him anything? If he would say that I* "*owed him 2d. I would pay him 4d.* But he could not demand a "Farthing. And one Capt. *Levcrook* sitting by, asked him, *For* "*what he had arrested us?* *L. S.* said, *For Contempts of the Law.* "The said Captain asked him, *Which Way we might be freed?* He "said, *No Way without conforming and paying the said Contempts,* "viz., *the Fines, Court Charges, and his Fees.* When I desired "the Favour of him but two Days to set my House in order, and "then we would go to Prison, he said, *He could not give us two* "*Hours:* Yet the Lord delivered us in such a Way, as our "Enemies cannot find out to this Day: Blessed be his Name "for ever! Through all which cruel Dealing we have very "greatly suffered.——Beside the Hazard and Danger we are in, "through the diligent renewing of his Writs again, unless some "timely and diligent Care be taken for the speedy preventing "thereof.

"*Richard Banks.*"

After this Manner, by repeated Prosecutions in the Ecclesiastical Court, were honest Men frequently molested, and *Excommunicated*, in consequence of which, Writs *de Excommunicato capiendo* were issued for imprisoning them: This appears by the foregoing Narrative to have been *Richard Banks's* Case, who yet doth not appear to have been actually imprisoned, though so violently pursued by one of the Officers of that Court; however, such repeated Attacks could not fail of putting the Prosecuted to great Trouble and Expence.

ANNO 1670.

In this Year, for Meetings held at *Brough*, in this County, Distress of Goods was made on several Persons, to the Amount of 90*l.* 14*s.* 6*d.* Among these was *Robert Huntington*, from whom four Cows and twenty-five Sheep were taken, and sold: A Concurrence of Disasters, which soon after happened to the Buyers of them, was much observed: One *Simson*, of *Sowerby*, who bought two of those Cows, died in a little Time, leaving the Cows to his Father, who also died soon after him. One *White*, of *Coldbeck*, bought another of them, through the Persuasion of his Wife, who said, *They might as well have her as another:* In a short Time after, she and her Child were found drowned in a Pond, where the Water was scarce deep enough to cover her as she lay. We think it but just to lay before our Readers the Fact of such remarkable Incidents, and leave them to form such a Judgment thereof, as from the Nature of the Case, when maturely considered, shall result.

Remarkable also, in this Year, was the Case of *Thomas Stordy*, against whom a Warrant was granted for distraining his Goods and Chattels for 20*l.* 10s., for a Meeting at *Moorhouse*, though himself was then in Prison, and had been so near eight Years, under Sentence of *Premunire*, for not Swearing, and all his Estate had been seized for the King. But it pleased God to * release him

* Note, *Thomas Stordy* and *Stephen Pearson* were set at Liberty, after about ten Years' Imprisonment, by the King's Letters Patent in 1672.

from so long Captivity, by Means of *Charles Howard*, Earl of *Chester*, through whose Intercession, also, the King granted his Estate back again to his Children.

In the same Year, for Meetings at *Settura*, Goods were taken by Distress, to the Amount of 2*l*. 2*s*. 8*d*. And for Meetings at *Uldaile*, to the Value of 8*l*. 7*s*., including the wearing Apparel and Bedclothes which were taken from *John Gardhouse*, a very poor labouring Man. About the same Time, *John Gill*, of *Gray-Southen*, being with others in the Burying-place at *Eaglesfield*, read a *Paper* of *Christian Advice*, written by *William Dewsberry*: For this he was fined 20*l*., and being unable to pay it, the same was partly levied on *Richard Fawcett* and *John Fearon*, from whom, and others, for Meetings at *Pardsay*, were taken, Corn, Cattle, and other Goods, to the Value of 35*l*. 11*s*.

ANNO 1673.

Taken from several Persons, for a Meeting at *Tuthill*, in the Parish of *Coldbeck*, Goods worth 43*l*. 19*s*. 2*d*.

Thomas Bewley, of *Holtcliff-Hall*, aged about seventy-eight, was prosecuted by *Arthur Savage*, Priest, for 3*l*. Prescription Money, and had taken from him his Feather Bed, Bedclothes, and a Cupboard, worth 5*l*. The Hardship of the poor old Man's Case so affected the Neighbourhood with Compassion, that when the Bayliff exposed those Goods to Sale, no Body would Buy them at any Rate: Whereupon the Priest sued the Bayliff, and made him pay both his Demand and his Costs.

ANNO 1674.

On the 1st of *November* this Year, the same Priest again prosecuted the said *Thomas Bewley* for Tithe of Wool, Lambs, *&c.*, and notwithstanding his very great Age, sent him to Prison.

In this and the next preceding Year, were taken in this County for Tithes, in Corn and other Things, to the Value of 270*l*. 13*s*. 5*d*.

ANNO 1675.

In this Year were taken from *John Howe*, of *Newtown*, and others, for a Meeting at his House, Goods worth 57*l*. 16*s*.

ANNO 1676.

On the 20th of the Month called *January* this Year, *Thomas Bewley*, son of old *Thomas Bewley* aforesaid, and * *Alice Nicholson*,

* This *Alice Nicholson* was a poor Widow, with six Fatherless Children, whose Husband had died in Prison at the same Priest's Suit.

of *Woodhouse*, Widow, were committed to Prison on an *Exchequer* Process, at the Suit of *Arthur Savage*, Priest of *Coldbeck*; at which Time also *George Bewley*, an elder Son of the same ancient Man, was detained in Prison by the same Priest, where he had then lain about two Years. In the same Year, *John Strickett*, of *Branthwait*, *William Scott*, of *Greenrigg*, and *Isabel Peacock*, of *Whalpey*, a Widow who had six fatherless Children, were also committed to Prison at the same Priest's Suit: As was likewise *Grace Stalker*, Widow, at the Suit of *John Monkhouse* for Tithes.

In this Year also, for a Meeting held at *Pardsey-Cragg*, were taken from *John Steel* and others, Goods worth 25*l.* 1*s.*

ANNO 1677.

On the 30th of *September*, *John Jackson*, of *Kirklinton*, was imprisoned on a Writ *de Excommunicato capiendo*, at the Suit of *Robert Priestman* for *Predial* Tithes.

ANNO 1679.

In this Year, sixteen Persons were taken by a Sessions Warrant, and committed to Prison, for Absence from the National Worship, *viz.*, *John Jackson*, *William Graham*, *Christopher Taylor*, *Christopher Jackson*, *Humphry Tweedal*, *Fergus Watson*, *Andrew Taylor*, *Francis Gillespy*, *Thomas Vowe*, *George Graham*, of *Rigg*, *Andrew Hetherington*, *Simon Armstrong*, *James Clark*, *Henry Graham*, *George Graham*, of *Blackhouse*, and *John Scott*. And in the same Year, *William Langcake*, *T. Ostell*, *William Saul*, and *John Waite*, were imprisoned for Tithes at the Suit of *William Dalston*.

ANNO 1680.

The Amount of the Tithes, taken in kind from this People in this County, in this and the four Years next foregoing, is 777*l.* 5*s.* 3*d.*

In this Year, also, for Meetings at their respective Houses, were taken from *Thomas Drewry*, of *Newland's Row*, Goods worth 11*l.*; from *Henry Scollick*, of *Newbiggen*, Horses and Cattle worth 26*l.*; and from *Edward Tyson*, of *Bickerthwaite*, Goods worth 19*s.* 7*d.*

In the same Year, *John Saul*, *Thomas Splatt*, *John Ostell*, and *John Barne*, suffered Distress of Goods for refusing to Swear when summoned to serve on Juries at the Mannour Courts: Also, *John Graham* and *John Bell* were fined for the same Cause.

Several others, dwelling at *Scotby*, were returned into the *Exchequer* for refusing to Swear, upon Convictions for Recusancy, on Statutes made against *Papists*, and suffered Distress of Goods on that Account, *viz.*:

		l.	s.	d.
Elizabeth Bond,	to the value of	5	19	7
Thomas Dobinson,	to the value of	6	0	0
John Richardson,	to the value of	3	17	8
		15	17	3

Some of those Goods were sold at low Rates in *Carlisle* Market, but when the People understood that they were the Spoils of Conscience, they refused to buy any more of them.

ANNO 1681.

In this Year, *John Aglionby*, a Justice of the Peace, was persuaded by *Jeremy Nelson*, Priest of *Stanwick*, to issue Warrants of Distress on several Persons for absenting themselves from the National Worship, by which Warrants Goods were taken to the Value of 8*l.* 9*s.* One of them was *George Gray*, a Man very poor, from whom the Spoilers took five Sheep-skins, which he had bought to clothe his Children, of whom he had several: One of the *Officers*, who made the Seizure, represented to the Priest the Hardship of the poor Man's Case, and his great Charge of Children, but the Priest's Answer to him was, *Let the Country maintain them.*

ANNO 1682.

On the 20th of the Month called *April* this Year, the following Persons were continuing Prisoners for Tithe, at the Suit of *Arthur Savage*, Priest of *Caldbeck, viz.*, *Thomas Bewley* and *Alice Nicholson*, who had then been Prisoners five Years and three Months; *William Scott*, five Years and four Months; *George Stalker*, four Years and four Months; and *Grace Stalker*, five Years and ten Months. Also, *John Sowerby*, who had been Prisoner three Years and seven Months, at the Suit of *Allan Smallwood*, Priest of *Graystock*, and *John Todhunter*, who had been imprisoned three Years and two Months, at the Suit of the same Priest. Also, *William Langcake*, *William Saul*, and *John Waite*, imprisoned three Years and three Weeks, at the Suit of *William Dalston*, Tithe-farmer. Likewise, *William Holme*, imprisoned above a Year on a Writ *de Excommunicato capiendo*, at the Suit of

William Stanley, of *Dalgarth*, Impropriator, died a Prisoner on the 2nd of *September* this Year. *Hugh Tickell* and *Thomas Birkhead* were Prisoners by Attachments out of the *Exchequer*, at the Suit of *Richard Lowry*, Priest of *Crossthwaite*. In this Year were discharged out of Prison, *Randolph Bulman*, committed on a Writ *de Excommunicato capiendo*, at the Suit of *Thomas Blemer*, Farmer of the Bishop's Tithe: Also, *John Slee*, who had been committed at the Suit of *Allan Smallwood;* and *George Bewley*, who had lain in Prison more than five Years, at the Suit of *Arthur Savage*, Priest of *Caldbeck*.

In *November* this Year, *John Holme* was committed to Prison at the Suit of *Lancelot Simpson*, Impropriator: Also, *Thomas Robinson*, *Matthew Stordy*, and *Thomas Bone*, were imprisoned after Excommunication, at the Suit of *Jeremy Nelson*, Priest: *Arthur Cordell* was also imprisoned six Weeks, at the Suit of *Rowland Nichols*, a Priest.

Anno 1683.

On the 13th of the Month called *February* this Year, several Informers came to a Meeting at *Pardsey Cragg*, and found *Peter Fearon* preaching: They applied to Justice *Fletcher*, who fined him 20*l.*, and ordered the same to be levied on himself and several others present, although the said *Peter* desired him to charge the Whole on himself, he being of sufficient Ability, but the Justice would not. In a short Time after were taken by Distress for the said Fine,

	l.	*s.*	*d.*
From *Peter Fearon*, Goods worth	5	5	0
,, *Allan Peile*, an Horse worth . . .	3	0	0
,, *John Banks*, Goods worth	7	4	0
,, *John Tiffin*, two Cows worth . . .	5	10	0
,, *John Fallowfield*, Goods worth . .	7	0	0
	27	19	0

When these Goods were exposed to Sale, and Buyers of them could not be found, the Justice ordered his own Servants to purchase some of them, which they did at a very low Price, and the Officers, to supply the Defect, made another Seizure on some of the Persons concerned.

For a Meeting at *Crossfield*, in the Parish of *Cleater*, were taken from *John Nicholson* two Oxen, worth 8*l.*, and from *Thomas Sharp*, of *St. Bees* Parish, two Oxen, worth 6*l.* 6*s.*

Christopher Story, of *Righead*, for permitting a Meeting at his House, had taken from him, by a Warrant granted by Justice *Aglionby*, two Horses, worth 5*l.* 10*s.*

ANNO 1684.

In the Month called *May* this Year, *Thomas Stordy*, *William Johnson*, *John Robinson*, *Japhet Allason*, *Joseph Steel*, *John Banks*, and *John Bewley*, of *Gateskail*, were Prisoners in *Carlisle* Gaol: And in the same Year, *Richard Ribton*, *Jonathan Bowman*, and *Thomas Hall*, all of *Broughton*, were imprisoned for refusing to pay small Tithes, at the Suit of *Richard Tickel*, Priest of *Bridekirk*. Also, in the Month called *January* this Year, *Christopher Fearon*, *Richard Head*, *John Robinson*, *Thomas Robinson*, and *Anne Steel*, Widow, all of *Messer*, and *Luke Steel*, of *Mersgill*, were committed to *Carlisle* Gaol, by an *Exchequer* Writ, for Tithes, at the Suit of *George Fletcher*, of *Hutton*. About the latter end of the Month of *December*, *Thomas Stordy* died a Prisoner, having continued stedfast through manifold Sufferings to the end of his Pilgrimage.

Taken this Year for Fines on the Conventicle Act,

	l.	*s.*	*d.*
From *William Graham*, of *Riggfoot*, Corn worth . .	0	5	6
,, *Christopher Taylor*, of *Hetherside*, Rye worth	0	5	0
,, *Christopher Story*, of *Righead*, Sheep worth .	1	8	0
,, *Henry Graham*, Oats worth	0	15	0
	3	3	6

On the 17th of the Month called *February* this Year, was a Meeting of Women at *Pardsey-Cragg*, to which three Justices came, and demanded of them, *What they met there for?* One of the Women answered, *To take Care of the Poor:* Which was indeed the Occasion of their Meeting. One of the Justices asked, *Whether there were no Beggars among them?* To which they answered, *No.* He replied, *That is well.* Nevertheless, the Justices turned them out of the House, and fined some of them as being at an unlawful Assembly: For which Fines, *Elisabeth Tolson* and *Mary Wilson* suffered Distress of Goods to the Value of 12*s.*

Thomas Scott, of *Ousebride-End*, for refusing to take an Oath at the Mannour Court, suffered Distress of Brass and Pewter to the Value of 4*l* 8*s.*; and *John Roger*, of *Water-End*, had for the same Cause his Pewter taken away, to the value of 8*s.* Also,

John Caipe, of *Uldall*, for not procuring a Person to swear that his Wife was buried in Woollen, though divers were ready to attest it, had his Goods taken by Distress, to the Value of 2*l*. 10*s*.

ANNO 1685.

William Adcock, of *Sunderland*, was fined at a Mannour Court for refusing to Swear, and had taken from him Goods worth 15*s*.

Christopher Taylor, *Andrew Taylor*, *William Graham*, *Henry Graham*, *George Blair*, *Andrew Graham*, *Philip Hassard*, *Richard Latimer*, *Andrew Hetherington*, *Simon Armstrong*, and *Christopher Story*, for being at a Meeting, were indicted at the Assizes as Rioters, and for not traversing that Indictment, sent to Prison.

ANNO 1687.

On the 8th of the Month called *March* this Year, *Elizabeth Watson*, of *Highmore*, Widow, died a Prisoner for Tithes, at the Suit of *George Fletcher*, Impropriator.

ANNO 1688.

In this Year were remaining Prisoners in *Carlisle* Gaol, at the Suit of *George Fletcher*, Impropriator, *Japhet Allason*, *Luke Steel*, *John Seenhouse*, sen., *John Seenhouse*, jun., *Joseph Steel*, *Christopher Fearon*, *Anne Steel*, *John Banks*, and *William Wright*; and at the Suit of *John Lowther*, of *Lowther*, Impropriator, *Thomas Ostel*, *Mary Saul*, Widow, *William Glaister*, *Thomas Drapp*, *Anthony Skelton*, *William Bouch*, *Arthur Skelton*, *John Biglands*, and *Thomas Wilkinson*.

ANNO 1689.

The generality of the People called *Quakers*, imprisoned in this County, were set at Liberty by Means of an Act of Grace granted by King *William* and Queen *Mary*, after their Accession to the Crown.

ANNO 1690.

By the Accounts of Tithes taken from the said People in this County, from 1681 to 1690, it appears, that the Value of Corn and other Things taken in Kind, amounted, within those ten Years, to the Sum of 2,215*l*. 15*s*. 9d. And that in three of those Years the Sums taken from them for Steeple-house Rates and Clerks' Wages, amounted to 3*l*. 13*s*. 6*d*.

WESTMORLAND.

ANNO 1651.

In this Year *Christopher Bisbrown*, of *Arnside*, was convinced of the Truth, as professed by the *Quakers*, and being at that Time Churchwarden of the Parish, had a conscientious Scruple of acting in that Office, and forbore to collect the Moneys called *Church-Dues*, for which Neglect he had Goods taken from him worth 5s.

ANNO 1656.

Thomas Alexander and *Christopher Hebson*, for some Opposition to one of the Priests, were imprisoned at *Appleby*, where they were cruelly beaten and abused by the unmerciful Gaoler, insomuch that the said *Richard Hebson*, being put out of Prison, in a few Days after died of the Hardships there received.

Thomas Taylor, *Christopher Taylor*, and *Anne Airey*, were imprisoned in the same Gaol for speaking to one of the Priests. The said *Christopher Taylor* gave forth in Writing a *Representation* of the Usage they met with there, which he directed to the Officers and Magistrates.

ANNO 1660.

In this and some preceding Years were taken for Tithes demanded from divers Persons in this County, amounting to 36*l.* 8*s.* 5*d.*, Cattle, Corn, and other Goods worth 140*l.* 12*s.* 4*d.* Also for Claims of *Church-Rates* and *Easter-Offerings*, amounting to no more than 9*s.*, Goods to the Value of 1*l.* 6*s.* 4*d.*

William Hebson, for his conscientious Refusal to pay Tithes, suffered forty Weeks' Imprisonment: And *John Fothergill*, for the same Cause, was imprisoned fourteen Months: *William Cartmell* and *Mabell Camm* were also imprisoned for the same Cause.

Richard Sill, *Edward Robinson*, *Thomas Robertson*, *Thomas Atkinson*, *Henry Ward*, *Thomas Wright*, and *Isabel Garnet*, were prosecuted in the *Exchequer* for refusing to pay Tithes. Also, *Robert Story*, of *Birkrigg-Park*, was sued at Common Law by

Edward Wilson, of *Dallan-Tower*, Esq., for seven Years' Tithe, and suffered the Loss of more than 50*l.*

Arthur Burrow, *Thomas Sill*, *Richard Sill*, and *Daniel Tompson*, all of *Preston-Patrick*, *Robert Atkinson*, of *Birkrigg-Park*, *Edward Burrow*, of *Lapton*, *Richard Parke*, of *Wood-house*, and *William Cartmell*, of *Warth-Sadden*, were all taken from their own Houses by Order from Captain *John Lowther;* and upon their Refusal to take the Oath of Allegiance, were committed to Prison, some at *Kendal*, and others at *Appleby*, where they continued several Weeks.

The Number of Prisoners at *Kendal* was shortly afterwards enlarged by the Commitment of *Robert Story*, *John Audland*, *James Sill*, *Henry Horseman*, *John Middleton*, *William Story*, *Charles Story*, and some others, who, being taken at a Meeting at *Birkrigg-Park*, and carried before *Allen Bellingham*, Justice, he tendred them the Oath, and upon their Refusal to take it, committed them to Prison.

About the same Time, *Henry Ward*, *Thomas Robertson*, *Peter Moser*, *Edward Fawcet*, *James Beck*, *Allen Wilson*, *James Rowlandson*, *William Farrer*, and *Thomas Ayrey*, of *Blakethwaite*, having been at a Meeting at the said *Henry Ward's* House, were taken before *James Duckett*, of *Grayrigg*, a Justice of the Peace, who tendred them the Oath of Allegiance, and upon their refusing to take it, committed them to *Appleby* Gaol, where they were detained till the next Quarter Sessions.

ANNO 1661.

Jane Johnson, of *Stubbe*, Widow, after a Prosecution in the *Exchequer* for Tithes, had her Goods taken away to the Value of 40*l.* *Isabel Garnet*, for Tithe of four Acres, had Goods taken from her to the Value of 40*s.* *John Dickenson*, of *Grayrigg*, was several Times imprisoned, and put to more than 10*l.* Charge, for not paying Tithes.

Peter Moser, of *Grayrigg*, was imprisoned for a trivial Sum demanded for an *Easter-Offering*, at the Suit of *William Brownswood*, Priest of *Kendal:* He remained in Prison till the Parson had prevailed on the Affection of his Mother to pay 40*s.* for his Discharge.

ANNO 1662.

The three Persons next under-named were taken at a religious Meeting on the 14th of the Month called *July*, and constrained to appear at the Quarter Sessions at *Appleby* the next Day, where they were fined, and by Order of Court shortly after had Goods taken as follows, *viz.:*

	l.	s.	d.
William Hobson, for a Fine of 5l., two Cows worth . .	7	0	0
John Boulton, for a Fine of 5l., Leather worth	6	0	0
Michael Langhorne, for a Fine of 4l. 10s., two Cows worth	5	0	0
For Fines of 1l. 10s. Taken	18	0	0

At the same Sessions, *Thomas Langhorne* was fined 5l., and *Robert Hutchinson* 4l., and both of them were committed to Prison for Non-payment.

Christopher Bisbrown, for 6d. claimed for a Church-Rate, had Goods taken from him to five Times that Value.

ANNO 1663.

William Cartmell, for a Demand of 7s., *Richard Thompson*, for 2s., and *Arthur Burrow*, for 5½d. demanded for Tithes, were cast into Prison, at the Suit of *Richard Brown*, Priest of *Barton*, and were continued Prisoners thirty-three Weeks.

Taken this Year from *Christopher Bisbrown*, for 4s. 4d. claimed for Church Dues, Goods worth 12s. 6d.

About the same Time, *Elizabeth Story*, a Widow, of *Preston-Patrick*, was prosecuted for 1½d., demanded for Communicant-Money by *Richard Brown*, Priest of *Barton*, for which trifling Claim she was put to an Expence of 4l.

About the End of the Month called *July* this Year, *Francis Howgill*, being in the Market-place at *Kendal* about his ordinary Business, was summoned by the High-Constable to appear before the Justices, then sitting at a Tavern, who tendred him the Oath of Allegiance, and committed him to Prison till the Assizes to be held in the next Month at *Appleby:* Being brought thither the Oath was again tendred him, and upon Refusal to take it, an Indictment was drawn up against him, which he traversing, had Liberty till the next Assizes to answer thereto. Accordingly, at the following *Lent* Assizes he appeared, where Sir *Philip Musgrave*, a violent Man, endeavoured to incense the Judges against him as *a dangerous Person, a Ringleader of the* Quakers, *and a great Upholder of their Meetings.*

On the 19th of *October*, fifteen Friends were taken at a Meeting in the House of the Widow *Cocke*, at *Birkhagge*, for which they were afterward indicted at the Sessions, and several of them fined. Three of them, *John Ayrey*, *Robert Barrow*, and *Brian Lancaster*, were committed to Prison, where they lay above eleven Months.

On the 8th of *November*, *Anthony Bownas*, *Nicholas Denkin*, *Robert Bowman*, and *Thomas Sourby* were forced from a religious Meeting, and committed to Prison; as were, on the 22nd of the same Month, *John Morland*, *Edward Guy*, *John Salkeld*, *John Brown*, and *John Kendal;* and on the 29th of the same, *John Bolton*, *William Hebson*, *Thomas Langhorn*, *Robert Robinson*, *Thomas Langhorn*, jun., and *George Denison:* On the 6th of *December*, *Robert Hutchinson*, *William Berwick*, *George Berwick*, *Edward Winter*, and *Thomas Smith;* and on the 13th of the same, *William Fallowfield*, *William Bland*, *Richard Ayrey*, and *Henry Bowman*. At the next Sessions, in the Month called *January*, they were all fined, and generally had their Goods distrained. But the said *William Hebson*, *John Bolton*, and *Thomas Langhorn*, having been before fined for a first Offence, were now fined for the second Offence, and it was thought the Magistrates had an Intention of proceeding to banish them, if taken the third Time.

On the 28th of *December*, *Edward Robinson* was taken at a Meeting, and committed to Prison, at the Sessions fined 40*s*., and for Non-payment committed to the House of Correction three Months.

On the 13th of the Month called *March*, 1663–4, *Anthony Bownas*, *William Fallowfield*, *Thomas Langhorn*, *Thomas Langhorn*, jun., *Robert Winter*, *Henry Bowman*, *George Dennison*, *John Hobson*, and *Thomas Hobson*, being assembled to worship God, were taken out of their Meeting, and carried before a Justice of the Peace, who made a *Mittimus*, and sent them from Constable to Constable, to the County Gaol: Whither also *Lancelot Fallowfield* and *John Ayrey* had been sent on the 10th of the same Month.

Anno 1664.

Miles Walker, of *Middleton*, for a Demand of 1*l*. 13*s*. for Tithes, had Goods taken from him worth 12*l*. Also *Robert Atkinson*, of *Middleton*, had taken from him for Tithes, two Mares, two Caldrons, and six Pewter Platters, worth 10*l*.

In this Year *Christopher Bisbrown* was sued for Tithes to an Outlawry, and taken up on a Commission of Rebellion, by *Robert*

Wilkinson, a Bayliff of *Kendal*, at the Suit of *James Duckett*, of *Grayrigg:* The Plaintiff, instead of having him carried up to *London*, as the Writ required, to appear personally in the Court of *Exchequer*, found Means to keep him close Prisoner in the Bayliff's House above sixteen Months, endeavouring by that Means to force him to a Compliance: But the old Man, who was then seventy-seven Years of Age, bore his Confinement with *Christian* Patience, and at length died in the said Bayliff's House, the Place of his long Imprisonment.

Richard Burrough, of *Arnside*, Son-in-Law to the old Man last mentioned, was taken at the same time with his Father, and detained Prisoner in the said Bayliff's House two Years and nine Months.

Robert Story, of *Birkrigg-Park*, and *Thomas Pearson* and *John Pearson*, both of *Powbank*, were sued in the *Exchequer* for Tithes, at the Suit of *Thomas Briggs*, Priest of *Haversham*, and, upon a Commission of Rebellion, were attached by *Robert Wilkinson*, who was both Bayliff and one of the Commissioners. But after their Apprehension, it was discovered that the Priest had proceeded illegally against them, and that they had a manifest Advantage both against him and the Commissioners for their false Imprisonment: Nevertheless, they rendered not Evil for Evil, but freely forgave them, having learned the *Christian* Doctrine of *loving Enemies*, of *doing Good* to those that *hated* them, and *praying* for those who *despitefully used* and *persecuted* them.

In this Year *John Watson*, of *Thirmby*, had his Goods taken by Distress for his own and his Wife's not receiving the Sacrament, though his Wife was then dead. But it was not unusual with Informers to be guilty of such Mistakes. In this Year, also, *Miles Walker*, for 1*s*. 6*d*., demanded for an *Easter-Reckoning*, by *John Smith*, Priest of *Kirby-Lonsdale*, had Goods taken from him to the Value of 18*s*.

In our Relation of the last Year, we left *Francis Howgill* returned to Prison till another Assizes, which were in the Month called *August* this Year. At the Coming of the Judges, he caused two Papers to be presented them; one of them was a Declaration containing the Substance of the Oath, and the other a modest Defence of himself for refusing to Swear: Both which, he was informed, the Judges read. We shall, in the next Place, lay before our Reader

THE PROCEEDINGS AGAINST THE SAID FRANCIS HOWGILL, BEFORE JUDGE TURNER, AT THE ASSIZES AT APPLEBY, THE 22ND AND 23RD OF THE MONTH CALLED AUGUST, 1664.

Clerk.—*Bring* Francis Howgill *to the Bar.*

Judge.—*Here is an* Indictment *against you for refusing to Swear; you must plead* Guilty *or* Not Guilty.

F. H.—May I have Liberty to speak and make my Defence?

Judge.—*Yes, you may.*

F. H.—I will lay the true State of the Case before thee, seeing Judge *Twisden* is not here, who was privy to all the Proceedings hitherto against me. I was born and brought up in this County; my Carriage and Conversation is known, that I have walked peaceably toward all Men, as, I hope, my Countrymen can testify. About a Year ago, being in a neighbouring Market-Town, about my reasonable and lawful Occasions, I was sent for, by an High Constable, out of the Market to the Justices of the Peace, before whom I went: They had nothing to lay to my Charge, but fell to asking Questions to ensnare me about our Meetings, and when they could find no Occasion, they seemed to tender me the Oath of Allegiance, though they never read it to me, nor did I positively deny it; yet they committed me to Prison. At the next Assizes Judge *Twisden* declared that my *Mittimus* was *insufficient*: Nevertheless, he there tendred me the Oath, and engaged me to appear the next Assizes after, which I did, and then refusing to give Bond for the good Behaviour, and not to be present at any of our Meetings, I was committed to Prison, where I have been these five Months, some of that Time under great Restraint, and my Friends not suffered to speak to me. Now as to the Oath, the Substance thereof, with the Representation of my Case, is already presented to the Court, unto which I have set my Hand, and shall in those Words testify the same in open Court, if required; and seeing it is the very Substance of what the Law doth require, I desire it may be accepted, and that I may be cleared from my Imprisonment.

Judge.—*I am come to execute the Law; and the Law requires an Oath, and I cannot alter it: Do you think the Law must be changed for you, or only for a few? If this be suffered, the administration of Justice is hindred; no Action can be tried, nor Evidence given for the King: Your Principles are altogether inconsistent with the*

Law and Government: I pray you shew me which Way we shall proceed: Shew me some reason, and give me some Ground.

F. H.—I shall. In the Mouth of two or three Witnesses every Truth is confirmed, and we never denied to give, and still are ready to give Evidence for the King in any Matter for the ending of Strife between Man and Man, in Truth and Righteousness, and this answers the Substance of the Law.

Judge.—*Is this a good Answer, think you? Whether to be given with an Oath or without an Oath? The Law requires an Oath.*

F. H.—Still Evidence may be given in Truth, according to the Substance of the Law, so that no Detriment cometh unto any Party, seeing true Testimony may be born without an Oath; and I did not speak of changing the Law: Yet seeing we never refused to give Testimony, which answereth the End and Substance of the Law, I thought it reasonable to receive our Testimony, and not to expose us to such Sufferings, seeing we scruple an Oath only on a conscientious Account, for fear of breaking the Command of Christ, the Saviour of the World, which if we do, there is none of you able to plead our Cause for us with Him.

Judge.—*But why do you not go to Church, but meet in Houses and private Conventicles, which the Law forbids?*

F. H.—We meet together only for the Worship of the true God in Spirit and in Truth, having the primitive *Christians* for our Example, and to no other End but that we may be edified, and God glorified, and where two or three are met together in the Name of Christ, and He in the Midst of them, there is a Church.

Judge.—*That is true: But how long is it since you have been at Church, or will you go to the Church the Law doth allow of? Give me some Reasons why you do not go.*

F. H.—I have many to give, if thou hast Patience to hear me. 1*st*, God dwells not in Temples made with Hands. 2*dly*, The Parish-house hath been a Temple for Idols, and I dare not have Fellowship with Idols, nor worship in Idols' Temples; for what have we to do with Idols, their Temple, or Worship?

Judge.—*Were there not Houses called the Houses of God, and Temples?*

F. H.—Yes, under the Law, but the *Christians*, who believed in Christ, separated from these, and the Temple was made, and left desolate; and from the *Gentiles'* Temple too, and met together in Houses, and broke Bread from House to House, and the Church was not confined then to one particular Place, neither is it now.

Judge.—*Will you answer to your* Indictment?

F. H.—I know not what it is. I never heard it, though I often desired a Copy.

Judge.—*Clerk, read it.*

The *Indictment* was read, importing, that *he had wilfully, obstinately, and contemptuously denied to Swear, when the Oath was tendred.*

F. H.—I deny it.

Judge.—*What do you deny?*

F. H.—The *Indictment.*

Judge.—*Did you deny to Swear?*

F. H.—I gave unto the Court the Substance of the Oath, as you all know: I also told you, that *I did not deny it out of Obstinacy or Wilfulness, neither in Contempt of the King's Law and Government,* for I would rather chuse my Liberty than Bonds, and I am sensible it is like to be a great Damage to me: I have a Wife and Children, and some Estate, which we might subsist upon, and do Good to others: And I know all this lies at Stake, but if it were my Life also, I dare not but do as I do, lest I should incur the Displeasure of God; and do you judge, I would lose my Liberty wilfully, and suffer the Spoiling of my Estate, and the Ruining of my Wife and Children, in Obstinacy and Wilfulness? Surely not.

Judge.—*Jury, you see he denies the Oath, and will not plead to the* Indictment, *only excepts against it because of the Form of Words, but you see he will not Swear, and yet he says he denies the* Indictment, *and you see upon what Ground.*

Then the Gaoler was called, and gave Evidence, that *the Oath was tendred to him at a former Assizes, which he did refuse to take.*

So the Jury, without going from the Bar, gave in their Verdict *Guilty*, and the Court broke up for that Night.

The next Day, toward Evening, he was again brought to the Bar to hear his Sentence.

Judge.—*Come: The* Indictment *is proved against you: What have you to say, why Sentence should not be given?*

F. H.—I have many Things to say, if you will hear them. 1*st*, As I have said, I deny not Swearing out of Obstinacy or Wilfulness, but am willing to testify the Truth in this Matter of Obedience, or any other Matter wherein I am concerned. 2*ndly*, Because Swearing is directly against the Command of Christ. And, 3*rdly*, Against the Doctrine of the Apostles. 4*thly*, Even of some of the principal Members of the Church of *England*, as Bishop *Usher*, sometime Primate of *Ireland*, who said in his Works, that *the* Waldenses *denied all Swearing in their Age, from that Command of* Christ, *and the Apostle* James, *and that it was a sufficient Ground.* And Dr. *Gauden*, late Bishop of *Exeter*, in a Book of his I lately read, cites many ancient Fathers, proving, that *the* Christians, *for the first three Hundred Years, did not Swear*, so that it is now no new Doctrine.

Judge.—*Surely you mistake.*

F. H.—I have not their Books here.

Judge.—*Will you say, upon your honest Word, they denied all Swearing ?*

F. H. —What I have said, is true.

Judge.—*Why do you not come to Church, and hear Service, and be subject to the Law, and to every Ordinance of Man for the Lord's Sake ?*

F. H.—I am subject : And for that Cause do we pay Taxes, Tribute, and Custom, and give unto *Cæsar* the Things that are his, and unto God the Things that are His, *to wit*, Worship, Honour, and Obedience : But if thou meanest the Parish Assemblies, I tell thee faithfully, I am persuaded, and that upon good Grounds, that their Teachers are not the Ministers of Christ, nor their Worship the Worship of God.

Judge.—*Why, it may be, for some small Thing in the Service you reject it all.*

F. H. ——First of all, it is manifest they are *Time-servers*, one while preaching up that for *Divine Service* to the People, which another while they are crying down as *Popish*, *Superstitious*, and *Idolatrous*, and that which they have preached up twenty Years together, they make Shipwreck of all in a Day, and now again call *Divine*, and would have all compelled to that themselves once made void.

Judge.—*Why, never since the King came in.*

F. H.—Yes, the same Men that preached it down once, now cry it up, and are so stable and unwavering, that we cannot believe they are the Ministers of Christ. *2ndly*, They teach for Hire, and live by forced Maintenance, and would force a Faith upon Men contrary to Christ's and the Apostle's Rule, who would have *Every one persuaded in their own Minds*, and said, *Whatsoever is not of Faith, is Sin:* And yet they say, *Faith is the Gift of God, and we have no such Faith given*, and yet they will force theirs upon us, and if we cannot receive it, they cry, *You are not subject to Authority and the Laws.* And nothing but Confiscations, Imprisonment, and Banishment, is threatned; and this is their greatest Plea: I could descend to more Particulars.

Judge.—*Well, I see you will not Swear, nor conform, nor be subject, and you think we deal severely with you; but if you would be subject, we should not need.*

F. H.—Yes, I do so think indeed, that you deal severely with us for Obedience to the Command of Christ. I pray thee, *Canst thou shew me that any of these People for whom the Act was made, have been proceeded against by this Statute?* though I envy no Man's Liberty.

Judge.—*Oh, yes, I can instance you many up and down the Country that are* Premunired. *I have pronounced Sentence myself against divers.*

F. H.—What, against the *Papists?*

Judge.—*No.*

F. H.—What, then, against the *Quakers?* So I have heard, indeed. It seems, then, that Statute, which was made against the *Papists*, thou lettest them alone, and executest it against the *Quakers.*

Judge.—*Well, you will meet in great Numbers, and do increase, but there is a new Statute, which will make you fewer.*

F. H.—Well, if we must suffer, it is for *Christ's* sake, and for Well-doing.

The Judge then pronounced Sentence, with a faint and and low Voice, thus:

You are put out of the King's Protection, and the Benefit of the Law. Your Lands are confiscate to the King during your Life, and your Goods and Chattels for ever, and you are to be Prisoner during your Life.

F. H.—Hard Sentence for obeying the Command of Christ; but I am content, and in perfect Peace with the Lord. And the Lord forgive you all.

Judge.—*Well, if you will be yet subject to the Laws, the King will shew you Mercy.*

F. H.—The Lord has shewed Mercy to me, and I have done nothing against the King, nor Government, nor any Man, blessed be the Lord, and therein stands my Peace, and it is for Christ's sake I suffer, and not for Evildoing.

So he returned to Prison, where he continued to the End of his Days.

In this Year the Mayor of *Kendal* caused the Goods of many Inhabitants of that Town to be distrained, for their Absence from the publick Worship; but when their Goods were exposed to Sale, the Neighbours would not buy them, nor could the Justices get them sold at any Rate, till, by bidding for them themselves, they animated some mean People to buy them at a very low Price. About the same Time *William Cartmell* and his Wife, *Edward Burroughs*, *Robert Atkinson*, *Rowland Warrier*, *William Mansergh*, and *Dorothy Lorimer*, were committed to Prison. Also, *Christopher Bisbrown*, of *Arnside*; *Miles Walker*, *John Thurnbeck*, and *Richard Walker*, of *Middleton*; *Dorothy Middleton*, and *John Middleton* her Son, had their Goods taken by Distress for Absence from the National Worship.

In or about this Year, many were fined for their religious Meetings, and committed either to the Common Gaol, or House of Correction, for one, two, or three Months, and some of them longer, *viz.*, *William Whitehead*, *Richard Barwick*, *John Barwick*, *James Fallowfield*, *William Bland*, *Edward Winter*, *Robert Winter*, *Eleanor Winter*, *Thomas Hobson*, *Mary Robinson*, *John Brown*, *Mary Ayrey*, *Thomas Langhorn*, *Thomas Smith*, *Jennet Smith*, *Anne Smith*, *Frances Lawson*, *Elizabeth Wilkinson*, *Elizabeth Holme*, *Ellen Cloudsdale*, *Jennet Atkinson*, *Agnes Whinfall*, *Margaret Fallowfield*, *Sarah Whitehead*, *Dorothy Ayrey*, *Margaret Bownas*, *John Boulton*, *Grace Whitehead*, *Isabel Whitehead*, *John Thompson*, *Michael Scaife*, *William Scaife*, *Henry Fisher*, *Richard Holme*, and *Anne Laycock*. Also, *Elizabeth Moreland*, Wife of *John Moreland*, who, while in the House of Correction, had a young Child sucking at her Breast. *Hugh Gibson*, a poor Man, who had been blind from his Birth. *Elizabeth Gibson*, the said blind Man's Sister, a very poor and weak Woman. *Katharine Clark*, a married Woman, with a sucking Child. *Jane Winter*, a Servant, the only Person left of a Family who were before in Prison. *Robert Hutchinson*, who also had his Clothes taken out of his Mother's House by one *Jackson*, an old Informer, without any Warrant appearing for so doing: When the Sufferer complained of that Injury to the Justices, he obtained no Redress. *Mary Holme*, a Woman then great with Child. And *John Robinson*, who was committed on a false Information, not having been at the Meeting he was accused of.

ANNO 1665.

Several of the Persons last before-named, were again this Year committed to Prison for a second Offence in meeting together.

In this Year, also, *John Beck*, then Mayor of *Kendal*, sent his Officers to summon all the *Quakers*, and other *Non-conformists* in the Town, before him, but none appeared, except twenty *Quakers*, seventeen of whom he fined 3*s*. each, and ordered the other three, *viz.*, *Thomas Holmes*, *Robert Barrow*, and *Brian Lancaster*, to be prosecuted on an old Indictment, and committed them to Prison, but after eight Days' Confinement, again discharged them, fining them 13*s*. 4*d*. each, for which their Goods were afterwards distrained.

In the same Year, *Thomas Burden*, of *Burden*, in the County of *Durham*, *William Park*, *Thomas Sill*, *William Chambers*, *Daniel Thompson*, and *Charles Story*, all belonging to *Preston* Meeting, were brought before *Allen Bellingham*, a Justice of the Peace, for being at a Meeting, and he committed the first four of them to the Common Gaol, and the two last to the House of Correction at *Kendal*, on the Act of Banishment, for the first Offence.

Josiah Coale, of *Winterbourn*, in the County of *Glocester*, was taken out of a Meeting at the House of the Widow *Johnson*, in *Preston-Richard*, by Order of the said Justice *Bellingham*, who committed him to Prison for three Months, on the Act for Banishment.

Morgan Watkins, of *Herefordshire*, was taken from the House of *Elizabeth Story*, Widow, and carried before *Daniel Fleming*, Justice, who committed him to Prison.

ANNO 1666.

William Hebson, for refusing to pay small Tithes, was imprisoned on a Writ *de Excommunicato capiendo*, above fifteen Months, and had also his Cattle taken away to the Value of 40*l*.

In this Year several Persons were fined by *James Ducket*, Lord of the Manour of *Grayrigg*, because they refused to Swear, and *Thomas Robertson*, for such Fine, had a Cow taken from him worth 3*l*. 6*s*. 8*d*.

Peter Moser, of *Grayrigg*, had also a Cow taken from him for a Fine, which Cow the said *James Ducket* killed, and salted in his own House for the Use of his Family.

ANNO 1667.

Richard Burrough, of *Arnside*, was prosecuted in the County Court for Tithes, at the Suit of *Elizabeth Ducket*, Widow and Executrix of *James Ducket*, deceased. She procured against him eight County-Warrants, the removing of which by *Certiorari* cost him 10*l*. 3*s*. 4*d*.

ANNO 1668.

Edward Burrough was prosecuted in *Beethom* Court, at the Suit of the said *Elizabeth Ducket;* and though that Court had no proper Jurisdiction in the Case of Tithes, yet they fined him 4*l*. 10*s*., for which the Bayliff next Day took a Cow and an Horse worth 7*l*.

The two Daughters and Executrixes of *Christopher Bisbrown*, deceased, were also prosecuted by the said *Elizabeth Ducket*, in the Manour Court of *Beethom*, for the same Tithe for which their Father had before suffered Imprisonment till Death. *Mary Bisbrown*, one of the Executrixes, was summoned to appear, and upon her Non-appearance, a Verdict of 6*l*. 10*s*. was obtained against her for thirteen Years' Tithes, and a Warrant granted for Distress on her Goods, but she being only a Servant, and having no Effects, the Prosecutrix 'was disappointed, and the other Executrix was out of their Manour or Jurisdiction. Soon after this, *Robert Barrow*, of *Kendal*, who had married *Margaret Bisbrown*, the other Executrix, was summoned into the Court at *Kendal*, by the said *Elizabeth Ducket*, upon the aforesaid Verdict obtained at *Beethom* Court, where he demurred to the *Jurisdiction* of the Court. Some Time after, he was again summoned to the said Court, and four Actions were brought against him, at the Suit of the said *Elizabeth Ducket*, and on the 2d Day of the Month called *March*, 1668, those Actions were tried, and a Verdict obtained against him for 4*l.* for eight Years, for which the Bayliffs took one Cow which cost him 4*l.* 5*s.*, and Hay valued at 15*s.*, also four Pewter Plates, five Brass Pans, and one great Kettle or Caldron. It was observed, that the said *Elizabeth Ducket*, and her Servant *Michael Langcake*, were very warm in this Prosecution, she declaring, that *She would spend* 100*l. upon the Executors of* Christopher Bisbrown; and he affirming, that *He would spend* 40*l. out of his own Purse, rather than that they should not be subjected to their Wills.*

John Bisbrown, for a Demand of 1*l.* 4*s.* for Tithes, had taken from him, at the Suit of the said *Elizabeth Ducket*, a Cow worth 3*l.*

Miles Bateman, the Elder, *Robert Barrow*, and *John Fell*, all of *Kendal*, were prosecuted in the Ecclesiastical Court at *Richmond*, for small Tithes and *Easter-Offeri gs*, at the Suit of *William Brownswood*, Priest of *Kendal*, and were committed to Prison, where the former remained five Weeks, and the other two nine Weeks: After which, they being informed of some Illegality in the Proceeding against them, appealed to the Ecclesiastical Court at *York*, upon which they were set at Liberty during the Appeal, and were likely to recover Charges of the Priest: But by the Advice of one Dr. *Burwell*, the Priest took an Oath of the Legality of his Prosecution, and thereupon they also were cited to take an Oath in the Cause, otherwise they would again incur a Contempt. But while these Matters were depending, both the Priest and Dr. *Burwell* died, having first put the said *Robert Barrow* and *John Fell* to about 7*l.* Charge, beside their false Imprisonment. The Apprehending of *Robert Barrow* in this Case, was attended with an ill-natur'd Circumstance: When the Bayliffs came to his House he was sick, and had taken Physick, wherefore he desired them to forbear taking him from Home till the next Day. The Bayliff accordingly applied to the Priest, telling him, that *It might endanger the Man's Health to take him away at that Time:* But the Priest churlishly answered, that *Unless he would pay, he should go immediately to Gaol.* So they hurried him away to the apparent Danger of his Health.

In the same Year, *John Bisbrown*, for a Claim of *Church-Dues*, amounting to 1*s.* 3*d.*, had Goods taken away worth 4*s.* 8*d.* And

Thomase Camm, of *Camsgill*, for a Demand of 1s., had Goods taken by Distress worth 2s. 6d.

ANNIS 1670 AND 1671.

After the coming forth of the second Act against Conventicles, the following Persons had their Goods taken by Distress, in Consequence of Warrants granted by the Justices, upon Informations of their being at religious Meetings, *viz.*, *Christopher Birket*, for permitting a Meeting at his House near *Kendal*, was fined 20l., for which the Constable took Beasts, Sheep, Horses, and Household Goods, and lockt up the Barn-doors, taking the Keys with him. The Woman of the House being sick, he took the Kettle off the Fire, and threw the Victuals out of Doors. From *Miles Bateman*, for preaching at that Meeting, for a Fine of 20l. they made a Seizure of two Kine, one Heifer, and eight or nine Acres of Corn: At another Time he was fined 20l. for permitting a Meeting at his House, and 10l. for his own being there, for which Fines they took nine Beasts, above fifty Sheep, and a Mare. A Justice of the Peace directed the Officers to sell the Goods for whatsoever was offered them, though never so little, and then to go again and take more, and lock up the Barn-doors. *Miles Hubersty*, for preaching at that Meeting, had above sixty Sheep, his Corn, Hay, and Household Goods taken away, the value of which much exceeded the Sum demanded, yet did the rapacious Spoilers threaten his Tenant for preventing them from taking more. *Dorothy Bateman* and *John Holme*, being fined 10s. each, they took from her Corn on the Mow, and from him his Bedding. From *Thomas Holme*, for a Fine of 5s., they took the Coat from his Back. From *Thomas Cooper*, for a Fine of 5s., they took Pewter, Brass, and other Goods worth 7 or 8s., and also an Heifer. From *Miles Halhead*, *Miles Hubersty*, and *Mary Pepper*, for Fines of 5s. each, they took from the *first* a Brass Pot, the *second* a Pair of Racks, and the *third* a Chair. For the like Fines they took from *Peter Bateman* a Rugg, *Dorothy Bateman*, Pewter worth 7s., *John Tompson*, a Pot worth 10s., *Richard Crewdson*, a Pair of Shoes, a Shirt, and other Things. And from *Roger Backhouse* a Parcel of Yarn. *Richard Holme* was not at the Meeting, yet was he fined on a false Information, as were several others, whom the Informers at random swore to be there. From *Thomas Graham*, for 10s. Fine for himself and Wife, they took Brass, Pewter, and other

Things. And from the Widow *Graham*, fined 10*s.* for herself and her Daughter, they took about thirty Yards of Cotton. For Fines of 5s. each, they took from *John Holme* three Kettles. *James Nuby*, a Pair of Sheerman's Sheers. And from *Elizabeth Kitchen*, a Brass Pot: At another Time they took from the said *Elizabeth Kitchen*, for a Fine of 10*s.*, Brass and Pewter worth 13*s.* From *Anthony Bownas*, of *Shapp*, for Fines of 2*l.* 15*s.* for himself and others, they took two Kine, one Steer, and a little Heifer, worth about 7*l.* And at several other Times, for Fines amounting to 2*l.* 15*s.*, they took Goods worth 3*l.* 6*s.* 4*d.* From *John Sutton*, of *Clifton*, they took a Caldron and a Brass Pot worth 14*s.* From *Thomas Savage*, of *Clifton*, for 1*l.* 5*s.*, they took Goods of twice that Value. From *William Whitehead*, of *Waters*, for 20*s.* for himself and *Thomas Langhorn*, they took four Stone of Wool worth 24*s.*

John Bolton, of *Bongate*, was at several Times fined 45*s.* for himself and others, which his Son, not of his Persuasion, being Constable, paid, rather than distrain his Father's Goods; though without his Father's Consent.

James Fallowfield, of *Great Strickland*, for 18*s.* 4*d.* for himself and *Elizabeth Smith*, had his Household Goods taken away to the Value of 4*l.* From *Edward Winter*, of *Moreland*, for 5*s.* Fine, they took a Rugg worth 10*s.* They also made Distress on *Lancelot Fallowfield*, of *Great-Strickland*, for 15*s.* Fine, but a young Man, who boarded with him, redeemed the Goods by paying the Fine. *Thomas Langhorn*, of *Hilton*, being fined 30*s.* for himself and others, they took from him a Cow worth 40*s.* From *Richard Simpson*, of *Bampton-Scarr*, for 10*s.* Fine, they took his working Tools, he being a Plaisterer. From *Thomas Langhorn*, jun., they took three Stone of Wool, and two Brass Pots, worth 1*l.* 6*s.* 8*d.* From *Christopher Wilkinson*, of *Tirrell*, and *Elizabeth* his Sister, for Fines of 10*s.*, they took wearing Apparel worth 40*s.* From *John Brown*, a Carpenter, of *Askham*, they several Times took away his working Tools. From *Robert Winter*, of *Moreland*, for 10*s.* Fine, they took a Mare worth 2*l.* 13*s.* 4*d.* From *William Muckeld*, of *Over-Stavely*, who was fined 20*l.* for a Meeting at his House, they took seven Beasts, two Horses, some Sheep, and fourteen Acres of Hay and Corn, wherein he was Partner with another Person, and sold his Part of them. From *Thomas Smith*, of *Sleagill*, for 40*s*. Fine, they took two young Beasts, worth 2*l*. 10*s*. From *Mary Holme*, of *Sleagill*, for 10*s*. Fine, Goods worth 16*s*. From *William Savage*, of *Clifton*, for 25*s*. imposed on him and *Christopher Wilkinson*, they took a Mare worth 2*l*. 7*s*. From *Lancelot Fallowfield*, for 40*s*. laid on himself and others, they took Goods worth 4*l*.

Christopher Wilkinson had goods taken from him worth 2*l*. 15*s*., for 40*s*. Fine imposed for himself and *Thomas Langhorn*, jun.

Edward Guy, of *Appleby*, was fined at several Times, for being at several Meetings, 5*l*. 5*s*., and for part of a Fine of the House where they met, was laid on him 6*l*. 10*s*. For the former of which Fines, they took Household Goods worth 9*l*. 15*s*., and for the latter they seized his Shop Goods, but did not carry them away.

William Whitehead, of *Waters*, was fined 3*l*. for being at several Meetings, for which they took from him at one Time, three Kine worth 9*l*., and at another Time, a Cow worth 2*l*.

John Dickinson, *Anne Ayrey*, and others, were also fined for being at Meetings in this County.

There was at this Time one *John Jackson* who acted the Part of an Informer on every Act against the *Quakers*; it was observed, that notwithstanding his ill-gotten Gain that Way, he was reduced to such extream Poverty as to beg his Bread.

Taken by Warrants granted by *Allen Bellingham*, Justice, from *Thomas Pearson*, the Elder, of *Wetherslack*, for a Fine of 20*l*. for a Meeting at his House, twenty-three Hides of tanned Leather; and from *John Pearson*, of the *Powbank*, for 10*s*. for himself and Wife, Goods of about that Value.

There were also fined, for being at the said Meeting in *Thomas Pearson's* House, several Persons who dwelt in *Lancashire*, viz., *Richard Simpson*, of *Cartmell*, for praying there, 20*l*., and *James Taylor*, *Richard Brittain*, *Laurence Newton*, *Christopher Fell*, and *John Barrow*, for being present, 5*s*. a piece, all which Fines were levied by Distress, and great Spoil and Havock was made of their Goods.

Several others who dwelt in this County, for being at the Meetings at *Sedbergh*, in *Yorkshire*, which they at Times frequented, were fined upon Convictions sent to *Henry Wilson*, a Justice near *Kirby-Lonsdale*, in this County, *viz*.,

	l.	s.	d.
Richard Walker, of Middleton, for himself and *Margaret* his Sister	1	0	0
James Corney, of Killington	0	15	0
Richard Parrot, of the same	0	15	0
Joseph Baines, of the same, for himself and for *Margaret Walker*	1	15	0
Robert Atkinson, of Middleton, for himself and *John Thirnbeck*	1	5	0
James Corney aforesaid, for himself and the said *John Thirnbeck*	2	15	0
Miles Walker, of Middleton	0	5	0
	8	10	0

ANNO 1672.

Thomas Robertson, of *Grayrigg*, was prosecuted for Seven Years' Tithe of Wool and Lambs, at the Suit of *John Archer*, and cast into Prison at *Kendal*, where he was kept fourteen Days, when some of his Relations, without his Knowledge, paid the Prosecutor 5*l*., and discharged him. He afterward expressed such Dislike of this seeming Kindness of his Friends, that his Persuasions induced them to promise not to offend him in that kind any more.

ANNO 1673.

Thomas Langhorn, of *Hiltondale*, was prosecuted in the Ecclesiastical Court for Tithes, by *Lancelot Hutchinson*, Priest of *Askham;* the Process went on unknown to him, who had never been summoned to appear, till a Certificate of Contumacy was issued: Upon this he appealed to the Bishop's Court at *York*, and was put to 10*l*. Expence to prevent his being sent to Prison.

Charles Story, of *Preston-Patrick*, was prosecuted for Tithe-Corn, at the Suit of *Thomas Wilson*, Tithe-farmer.

William Baines, of *Killington*, for a Demand of 5*s*. for Priest's Wages, had Goods taken from him worth 14*s*., and *Joseph Baines*, for a Demand of 4*s*., Goods worth 20*s*.

ANNO 1674.

Thomas Camm, of *Cammsgill*, was sued by *John Ormrod*, Priest of *Burton*, for small Tithes and Oblations, and by a Writ *de Excommunicato capiendo*, was cast into Prison, where he remained between two and three Years.

William Baines, of *Killington*, was cited into the Court at *Richmond* for a Claim of *Easter-Offerings*, and put to an Expence of 20*s*.

ANNIS 1675 AND 1676.

In the Year 1675, *Joseph Baines*, *John Hodgson*, and *John Yeates*, all of *Killington*, were prosecuted for *Easter-Offerings*, and the said *John Hodgson* also suffered Imprisonment for Tithes, at *Kendal*, thirteen Weeks, for a trivial Claim of two Lambs, and about six Fleeces of Wool.

In the same Year, *William Baines* and *Joseph Baines* were cited into *Richmond* Court, at the Suit of *John Wood*, Priest of *Killington*, for Wages by him demanded. Their Appearance there occasioned 10*s*. Charge to each of them, but before the Court-day came, in which their Answers were to have been given in, the Priest was taken sick, and died under much Trouble of Mind.

John Thirnbeck, of *Middleton*, for a small demand of Tithes, was prosecuted by *Thomas Green*, an Attorney, at the Suit of Sir *Thomas Strickland*, and was apprehended by a Writ of Rebellion after the Time of the Return of the Writ was expired. He was kept Prisoner by *John Holme*, a Bayliff, at his House in *Kendal*, several Weeks, when getting a sight of the Writ, he found that the Date of its Return had been scraped out, and another Date of the next Term put in, and sending to search the Record at *London*, found that there was no Writ returnable against him. The Attorney, detected of this treacherous Dealing, was enraged, and procured a fresh Writ against the said *Thirnbeck*, returnable on the 10th of the Month called *April*, 1676, and a few Days after that Time sent him up to *London*, about two Hundred Miles, with a Person of ill Morals to attend him, to which Person he gave Directions *to beat the Prisoner if he refused to go:* But by that Time they came to *Nottingham*, the Return of that Writ was also expired, and the Prisoner refusing to go any farther, his Guide, after some Abuses, left him.

Thomas Moore, of *Hutton-Roofe*, and *Dorothy Middleton*, of *Lupton*, were prosecuted in the Bishop's Court at *Richmond*, by *Henry Hogle*, Priest of *Kirby-Lonsdale*, for small Tithes, and in the latter End of the Year 1675, were cast into Prison by a Writ *de Excommunicato capiendo*, where they remained till the Priest died: After whose Death they were kept in Prison by *John Newton*, of *Kirby-Lonsdale*, the Priest's Proctor, till he also died, and then they were set at Liberty, after four Years and about seven Months' Imprisonment.

Thomas Camm, of *Camsgill*, was sued in the Year 1675, in a Court-Baron, held at *Preston-hall*, for 3*s*. for his Salary, and (the said *Thomas Camm* being then a Prisoner) a Verdict was obtained against him, by Virtue whereof *Richard Lucas*, a Bayliff, took from his House Goods worth 5*s*. 6*d*.

In these Years were taken by Justices' Warrants, for Absence from the National Worship,

	l.	*s*.	*d*.
From *Edward Winter*, of Moreland, Goods worth - - - -	0	9	0
John Shearman, of Sleasgill, Goods worth - - -	0	4	0
Mary Holme, of the same, Goods worth - - - -	0	6	0
Thomas and *Anne Robinson*, of Cliburne - - - -	1	4	0
William Barwick and *John Barwick*, of Shapp - -	0	6	0
Matthew Dawson, of Hilton, Goods worth - - -	0	5	6
Thomas Kendal, the Younger, of Askham - - -	0	7	6
Thomas Sutton, *Thomas Savage*, and *William Savage*, all of Clifton, Goods to the value of - - - - -	1	2	0
John Cleasby and *William Moorthwaite* - - - - -	0	18	0
James Scaife, of Nateby - - - - - - - - -	0	9	0
	5	11	0

ANNO 1677.

About this Time *Richard Thompson*, *Anne Thompson*, and *Arthur Burrow*, for 8*s*. demanded for his Salary by *Richard Robinson* Reader at *Preston* Chapel, had Goods taken from them by Distress, to the Amount of 1*l*. 7*s*. 6*d*.

In this Year *Thomas Williamson*, of *Bannerigg*, in the Parish of *Windermer*, having a Concern and Pressure upon his Mind to declare the Truth to the People assembled at the Steeple-house there, went thither, and tarried in Silence till *William Wilson*, the Priest, had ended his Sermon, after which he took an Opportunity to speak to the People what he had upon his Mind to declare. For this the Churchwardens, so called, at the Instigation of the Priest, complained against him to Justice *Flemming*, who, upon his refusing to give Sureties, committed him to Prison, where he lay till the next Sessions, and then was set at Liberty.

ANNO 1678.

In the Month called *April* this Year, was drawn up, attested by Witnesses, and presented to the Parliament,

"An ACCOUNT of the Names of such Persons, who are no
" *Papists*, but *Protestant* Dissenters, and distinguished by the

"Name of QUAKERS, and have been prosecuted upon the "Statutes of 23 and 28 of ELIZABETH, made against *Popish* "Recusants, and Levies for the Yearly Profits of their Lands "thereupon made by the Sheriff's Bayliffs of the said County, "by Process out of the *Exchequer* for the Year 1677, as "followeth, *viz.* :—

The Persons Names and Places of Abode.	*Yearly Value of Lands Seized.* l.	s.	d.		*Value of Goods Levied.* l.	s.	d.
James Clarkson, John Pinder, and *Anthony Robinson,* all of Ravenstondale - - - - - - -	1	19	4	..	4	12	0
Thomas Atkinson, of Orton Parish - - . -	1	0	0	..	2	0	0
Thomas Atkinson, William Whitehead, Richard Ayrey, John Clark, and *Richard Barwick,* all of Shapp Parish - - - - - - - - -	6	4	8	..	10	13	4
John Sutton, of Clifton - ; - - - - -	0	10	0	..	0	14	0
Edward Sutton, of Browham Parish - - - - -	0	5	0	..	0	9	0
Thomas Langhorn, of Hiltondale - - - - -	0	18	0	..	2	10	0
Richard Burrough, Jennet Besbrown, and *John Hudson,* all of Beethom Parish - - - - -	0	15	0	..	1	15	0
Bridget Gregg, of Milthorp - - - - - -	0	2	0	..	0	5	0
Edward Cragg, of Ackonthwaite - - - - -	0	0	8	..	0	6	0
John Pearson and *Thomas Pearson,* of Heversham Parish - - - - - - - - - - - -	2	0	0	..	3	10	0
Stephen Crossfield, of Heversham - - - - -	1	6	0	..	2	0	0
Thomas Ayrey, Robert Simpson, and *William Farrar,* all of Kendal Parish - - - - - - - -	3	6	0	..	5	2	0
Peter Moser, Robert Wilson, John Dickinson, Martin Simpson, and *Elizabeth Holme,* all of Kendal Parish - - - - - - - - - - - - -	1	15	2¼	..	3	18	0
Nicholas Suart and *William Elcray,* of Toutram	0	11	8	..	1	3	6
Richard Birket and *John Thompson,* of Crook - -	0	14	8	..	1	11	0
Miles Bateman of Underbarrow - - - - -	0	7	4	..	0	0	0
Richard Atkinson and *John Preston,* of Farleton -	0	12	0	..	2	6	7
George Denison, of Mansergh - - - - - -	0	4	8	..	0	10	0
	22	12	2¼		43	5	5

Many others also had their Goods seized by *Exchequer* Process in the Years 1677 and 1678, the Value of whose Lands are not mentioned, *viz.* :—

	l.	s.	d.
Henry Laycock, Thomas Lawson, Lancelot Fallowfield, James Fallowfield, Rowland Wilson, Nicholas Denken, John Hobson, and *Thomas Fallowfield*, all of Moreland Parish - - -	6	14	8
Mary Robinson, of Cliburne - - - - - - - - - -	0	6	8
Christopher Wilkinson, of Barton Parish - - - - - -	0	5	0
John Tinker and *Robert Hutchinson*, of Askham - - - -	1	8	0
Thomas Langhorn, of Hilton - - - - - - - - -	0	16	0
George Crossfield, of Stainton - - - - - - - - - -	0	4	0
Elizabeth Simpson, Isabel Fell, and *William Parke*, all of Docker	0	19	2½
Thomas Hudson, of the same - - - - - - - - -	0	4	0
William Chambers, of Sedgewick - - - - - - - - -	2	0	0
William Bisbrown, of Beethom Parish - - - - - - -	0	3	0
Dorathy Middleton, John Middleton, John Sutton, Edward Burrough, and *Henry Skyrigg*, all of Lupton - - - - -	1	9	0
Robert Atkinson, John Scaife, William Cartmell, and *Roger Wakefield*, all of Preston - - - - - - - - - -	1	1	8
Richard Stephenson, of Over-Stavely - - - - - - -	0	6	8
Riehard Clarkeon, Anthony Pinder, and *Thomas Fawcett*, all of Ravenstondale - - - - - - - - - - - - -	1	1	4
John Holme and *John Fawcett*, of Orton Parish - - - -	0	16	8
Michael Aiskell, of Brough - - - - - - - - - -	1	0	0
John Thompson and *William Scaife*, of Warcopp Parish - -	1	0	0
Robert Teasdale - - - - - - - - - - - - -	2	0	0
Edward Gray, of Appleby - - - - - - - - - -	5	6	8
John Bolton, of Bongate - - - - - - - - - -	0	10	0
	27	12	6½

In *November*, 1678, the following Distresses were made by the Sheriff's Bayliffs upon Process out of the *Exchequer*, *viz.* :—

	l.	s.	d.
From *Robert Simpson*, of Docker, a Cow worth - - - - -	3	6	8
Peter Mosser, of Greyrigg, Pewter and Brass worth - -	0	10	0
John Dickinson, of the same, Bed-clothes worth - - -	1	4	0
Martin Simpson, of the same, Goods worth - - - -	0	10	0
Thomas Ayrey, of Sellside, Pewter worth - - - - -	0	10	0
William Farrar, of Grayrigg, Goods worth - - -	0	6	8
Elizabeth Holme, Widow, Goods worth - - - -	0	8	0
John Thompson, of Crook, Goods worth - - - -	0	10	0
Miles Bateman, of the same, an Horse worth - - -	4	0	0
Thomas Pearson, of Powbank, an Heifer worth - - -	1	13	4
Nicholas Suart, of Toutram, an Horse worth - - -	4	13	4
William Elcray, of the same, Goods worth - - -	0	8	6

And in *September* the same year, had been taken

	l.	s.	d.
From *Edward Cragg*, of Ackonthwaite, an *Horse worth - -	3	10	0
Bridgett Gregg, of Milthorp, a Caldron worth - - -	1	0	0
Richard Atkinson, of Farleton, a Mare worth - - -	5	0	0
Richard Burrough, of Arnside, a Cart and Mare worth -	2	10	0
John Hudson, of Hale, a Cow worth - - - - - -	3	5	0
Jennet Bisbrown, of Arnside, Widow, Pewter worth - -	0	11	0
In *November* the same year, more			
From *John Pearson*, of Powbank, two Heifers worth - - -	2	6	8
Stephen Crossfield, of the same, a Cow worth - - -	2	10	0
	37	13	2

On the 5th of the Month called *June*, 1677, the Mayor of *Kendal* sent three Constables to the Meeting there, who found *Robert Barrow* preaching: At the next Sessions the said *Robert Barrow*, with *John Fell* and *Peter Jackson*, who were at the same Meeting, were indicted for a *Riot*, fined by the Court, and imprisoned a few Days: After which they had their Goods taken by Distress, *viz.*, from *Robert Barrow* to the Value of 16s., and from *John Fell* to the Value of 18s.

For a Meeting at *Bownass*, in the Parish of *Windermere*, on the 15th of *September*, 1678, several Persons were fined by *Daniel Flemming* and *Christopher Philipson*, Justices, and some Time after, by their Warrant, had Distresses made on them, and Goods taken worth £180. It happened at this Meeting, that certain rude Boys and others were very abusive, threw in a dead Dog, and behaved very insolently: which *John Thompson* observing, advised them to Sobriety and better Manners. This was sworn to be Preaching, and the Justices proceeded accordingly.

On the 13th of *October*, 1678, *Edward Wilson*, a Justice of the Peace, sent several Informers to a Meeting held in the House of *Edward Cragg*, of *Ackonthwaite*, in the Parish of *Haversham*, and upon their Evidence convicted divers Persons without being brought before him, and issued Warrants for Distress, by which was taken—

* This Horse was seized for a Demand of 8d. in the *Exchequer Roll*. A Neighbour, *Robert Gibson*, observing the unreasonableness of the Distress, redeemed the Horse, by depositing the Money.

	l.	s.	d.
From *Joseph Gregg*, a young Cow worth - - - - -	3	10	0
William Walker, a Mare worth - - - - -	4	5	0
Edward Cragg, Goods worth - - - - -	2	16	0
Simon Thompson and *George Wharton*, Goods worth -	1	10	0
Dorothy Lorimer and *Thomas Huggonson* - - -	0	14	10
Richard Thompson, of *Preston*, a young Heifer worth -	1	5	0
Thomas Camm, of *Camsgill*, for preaching at the said Meeting. nine Head of * Cattle, and fifty-five Sheep, worth - - - - - - - - -	31	10	0
Arthur Burrough, an Horse worth - - - -	3	6	8
Hugh Cornthwaite, an Heifer worth - - - -	2	16	0
John Hudson, a Cow worth - - - - -	0	5	0
Robert Waller, a Cow worth - - - - - -	3	12	0
Richard Atkinson, two Cows worth - - - -	7	5	0
John Preston, a young Steer worth - - - -	2	10	0
	68	5	6

ANNO 1679.

Taken for Tithes in Corn :—

From *Thomas Camm*, to the Value of - - - - -	4	5	4
Edward Cragg, of Actonthwaite - - - - -	2	9	0
Bridget Gregg, of Milthorp, Widow - - - -	0	5	0
Joseph Gregg, of the same, to the Value of - -	1	6	0
	8	5	4

ANNO 1680.

Taken for Tithe of Hay, from *Richard Atkinson*, of *Farleton*, for 4*s.* 2*d.* demanded, a Pair of Cart Wheels worth 16*s.* And from *Thomas Preston*, for a Claim of 12*s.*, Turf worth 18*s.*

Nicholas Thompson was prosecuted for Tithes at the Suit of Sir *Thomas Strickland*, and cast into Prison, where he lay five Months, and during his Imprisonment, the Prosecutor's Servants took from his Lands three Acres and a Half of Barley, worth 24*l.* *John Thirnbeck*, of *Middleton*, also suffered five Months' Imprisonment, at the Suit of Sir *Thomas Strickland.*

* When the Officers complained to Justice *Wilson*, that they could not sell some of the Cattle, he charged them to sell at any Price, and to fetch more till they had enough, and ordered them to go from one Market to another, and sell cheap, so as to encourage Buyers, and threatened them, that if they did not raise all the Fines, they should pay the rest out of their own Pockets.

ANNO 1681.

Joseph Baines, of *Killington*, and *John Thirnbeck*, of *Middleton*, being summoned to serve on a Jury at the Quarter-Sessions, appeared, but refusing to Swear, were fined 20*s.* each, and had their Goods taken away, the former to the Value of 40*s.*, and the latter of 2*l.* 10*s.*

Richard Atkinson, of *Farleton*, for 1*l.* 6*s.* 8*d.* demanded, being Two-thirds of his Yearly Estate, had taken from him, by the Statute made against *Popish* Recusants, two Kine worth 7*l.* 10*s.*

In this Year, *Richard Thompson*, of *Milnhouses*, *George Thompson*, *John Thompson*, *Robert Thompson*, *Richard Burkitt*, *John Dickinson*, *John Beck*, *William Elleray*, and *Nicholas Suart*, all of the Parish of *Kirby-Kendal*, were committed to Prison by Warrants granted by *Edward Wilson* and *John Fisher*, Justices, grounded on Certificates of Contumacy out of the Ecclesiastical Court, on Prosecution there for Tithes, where some of them remained Prisoners a long Time, and one of them, *viz.*, *William Elleray*, died a Prisoner there on the 28th of the Month called *August*, 1682.

ANNO 1682.

Reginald Holme, *John Dixon*, *William Rawes*, *William Harrison*, *Thomas Harrison*, and other Inhabitants of the Parish of *Grasmire*, in *Westmorland*, were prosecuted in the *Exchequer* for Tithes, at the Suit of *John Ambrose*, Vicar or Curate of that Parish. Sequestration was thereupon obtained, and by Virtue thereof, the Sequestrators, *George Garnet*, *William Fell*, and *George Mackreth*, entered the House of *William Rawes*, and took thence Brass, Pewter, Bedding, and his own, and his Wife's Apparel, to the Value of 6*l.*, leaving the poor Woman, then lying in Childbed, without Clothes necessary to keep her from the Cold, so that she was obliged to borrow of her Neighbours: One of the Sequestrators observing amongst the Spoil, which they carried away to an Alehouse about four Miles off, a Pair of new Shoes and Stockings, put them on, and left his old torn ones in their Place. On the next Day they came again, and broke open several Doors, and took what else they could find, to the Value of 4*l.* more. They also took away a Cow worth 3*l.* So that they took in all to the Value of 13*l.*, though the Tithe, demanded by the Priest, amounted at the most but to 2*s.* 6*d.* A grievous Oppression for a trifling Demand: But the Sufferers of such Spoil endured the same with the utmost Patience, esteeming the Peace of their Consciences above all outward Substance.

On the 6th of the Month called *August* this Year, a religious Meeting was held in the Barn of *Richard Atkinson*, of *Farleton*, of which Information being given to *Edward Wilson*, Justice, he sent Persons to observe who were there, and accordingly fined many of them, and granted a Warrant for Distress, dated the 15th of the same Month, by which were taken

	l.	*s.*	*d.*
From the said *Richard Atkinson*, two Oxen, a Cow, and five other Beasts, to the Value of - - - -	25	3	4
Thomas Preston, of Overforth, two young Steers worth -	5	0	0
James Fell, of Sedgewick, two Cows worth - -	7	0	0
Robert Waller, of Hale, a Cow worth - - -	3	10	0
Thomas Camm, of Cammsgill, two Oxen worth - -	7	0	0
Oliver Leigh, of Gatebeck, three Heifers worth - -	6	10	0
Charles Story, of Preston-Patrick, Goods worth - -	0	7	0
Richard Thompson, of Milnhouses, Brass worth - -	0	10	0
William Walker, of Milthorp, Goods worth - -	1	0	0
Thomas Atkinson, of the same, two Coats worth - -	1	0	0
Bridget Gregg, of the same, Flax and Candles worth -	0	9	4
John Watson, of the same, for his Wife - - -	0	5	4
Edward Cragg, of Ackonthwaite, Goods worth - -	0	9	6
Jane Swainson, a very poor Widow, a Bag of Potatoes provided for her Family, worth - - -	0	0	10
Thomas Jackson, of Barton in Kendal, Pewter worth -	0	6	0
Christopher Bisbrown, of Arnside, Hemp-Yarn worth -	0	5	7
	58	16	11

Several of the last-named Persons were fined on Account of a Preacher, who was said in the Warrant to be fled, and his Habitation unknown: Whereas the said Preacher was so far from flying, that he went to the Justice's House, and left Word there that his Name was *Thomas Docwra*, and that he dwelt at *Swarthmore*, near *Ulverston*, in *Lancashire*, and that he was of Ability to pay his own Fine, for which reason he desired it might not be imposed on others.

Eleven other Persons were also fined for being at the said Meeting.

ANNO 1684.

On the 5th of the Month called *April*, a Sequestration for Tithes, granted against *John Dixon*, was put in Execution, by which they seized his Cattle, Household Goods, and Apparel, to the value of 20*l.* But the said *Dixon's* Mother, one of the Priest's Hearers, made an Agreement with the Sequestrators, and took the Goods to herself, for 9*l.* 16*s.*, which she paid them.

In this Year 1684 many suffered Distress of Goods for Fines of 12*d.* per *Sunday*, for Absence from the National Worship, *viz.*:

	l.	*s.*	*d.*
Taken from *Richard Atkinson*, of Farleton, to the Value of -	0	16	0
Thomas Preston, of Oversworth, Goods worth - -	0	9	0
Edward Cragg, of Ackonthwait, and *Bridget Gregg*, of Milthorp - - - - - - - -	0	6	0
James Harrison and *James Fell*, both of Sedgewick -	0	11	8
Thomas Camm, of Cammsgill, and *Margaret Thompson*, Widow - - - - - - - - -	0	8	0
John Hudson and *Robert Walker*, both of Hale - -	0	19	6
William Jackson and *Richard Barrow*, of Arnside .	1	13	7
Thomas Jackson, of Burton, and *Thomas Huggonson* -	0	8	2
Richard Pye, of Storth, and *Thomas Williamson*, of Windermere - - - - - - - -	1	13	0
George Williamson, *William Williamson*, *Margaret Suart*, and *Miles Sawrey*, all of Windermere -	4	12	10
Isaac Dixson, *George Dixon*, and *John Braithwaite*, of the same - - - - - - - - -	2	0	6
George Thompson and *Elizabeth Blithe*, Goods worth -	0	9	8
Thomas Wilson and *Allen Wilson*, Leather worth -	0	18	0
Thomas Grave, *William Rawes*, *John Dixon*, and *John Rigge*, Wool worth - - - - - -	1	10	10
Dorothy Wilson and *John Walker*, Pewter worth -	0	16	0
Michael Wilson and *Thomas Harrison*, two Horses worth	4	0	0
Reginald Holme, *John Holme*, *Jacob Holme*, and *John Thompson*, Goods worth - - - - -	0	18	0
Robert Barrow, *Richard Holme*, and *Robert Newby*, all of Kendal, Goods worth - - - - - -	0	14	9
	23	4	9

For the same Cause of absenting from the National Form of Worship, *Christopher Bisbrown* and *Robert Harsden* were committed to Prison: And for the like Cause the Justices also committed several married Women to Prison, for the Act in that Case did not expressly authorise the Seizure of the Husband's Goods for the Wife's Offence: Under this Pretext were imprisoned, *Jane*, the Wife of *Richard Atkinson*; *Agnes*, Wife of *Thomas Preston*;

Elizabeth, Wife of *James Fell*; *Dorothy*, Wife of *Robert Lorimer*; *Alice*, Wife of *Richard Burrough*; *Agnes*, Wife of *George Williamson*; *Margaret*, Wife of *William Williamson*; and also the Wife of *Thomas Williamson*: Also, for the same Cause, *Elizabeth Braithwaite*, a young Maiden about seventeen Years of Age, was committed to Prison on the 6th of the Month called *July*, and remained there till she died, on the 26th of *September* following, after about eleven Weeks' Imprisonment. *Christopher Dixon*, a Servant, was also imprisoned for the same Cause.

For a Meeting at *Kendal*, in the Month called *July* this Year, was taken by Distress—

	l.	*s.*	*d.*
From *Robert Barrow*, *Thomas Copeland*, and *Robert Newby*, Pewter to the Value of - - - - - -	1	6	6
Israel Newby, his working Tools, worth - - -	0	8	8
Henry Fisher and *John Fell*, Pewter worth - -	0	18	0
George Taylor and *Thomas Wilson*, Goods worth - -	0	19	0
Bryan Lancaster had taken from him his Fine of -	0	5	0
	3	17	2

By virtue of the former the said Warrants were taken

	l.	*s.*	*d.*
From *John Hudson*, Cattle and Corn to the value of - - -	23	8	0
Robert Waller, Cattle and Corn to the value of - - -	11	4	0
Richard Atkinson, five Beasts and other Goods worth -	13	10	0
Jane Gregg, Pewter worth - - - - - - - - -	0	5	0
	45	7	0

And by the latter were taken

	l.	*s.*	*d.*
From *Richard Atkinson*, Cattle and Corn to the value of - -	39	14	0
James Fell, seven Head of Cattle worth - - - -	14	0	0
Thomas Moore, Oats worth - - - - - - - - -	2	5	6
Charles Story, Oats and Pewter worth - - - - -	0	18	6
Bryan Lancaster, a Parcel of tanned Hides worth - -	11	0	0
Margaret Thompson, Widow, Goods worth - - -	1	12	0
William Herdson, a poor Labourer, a Pewter Dish and six Spoons, not worth the Fine, amounting to - - -	0	3	0
Jane, Wife of *Joseph Gregg*, her Husband being then in Prison, Goods worth - - - - - - - -	0	12	0
Isabel, Wife of *John Hudson* - - - - - - -	0	10	0
Henry Skyring, of Lupton, whose Fine was paid without his Knowledge or Consent - - - - - - -	0	5	0
Simon Thompson, Goods worth - - - - - - -	0	10	0
	71	10	0

Also by Warrants granted by Sir *Daniel Fleming*, Justice, f
Meetings held at the House of *William Rawes*, in Langdale, wa
taken

	l.	s.
From *William Rawes*, Corn, Cattle, and Household Goods, worth - - - - - - - - - - - - -	14	0
John Dixon, Beasts, Hay, and Wool, worth - - - -	20	12
Michael Wilson, Goods worth - - - - - - - -	0	12
Thomas Harrison, Wool werth - - - - - - -	0	12
John Walker, four Oxen and an Iron Pot, worth - -	16	8
James Harrison, Goods werth - - - - - - - -	1	0
Dorothy Wilson, and *Rebecca* her Daughter, Goods worth	1	14
John Bigg, Wool worth - - - - - - - - - -	1	6
	56	6

Anno 1687.

James Fallowfield and *Lancelot Fallowfield*, of *Great-Stric land*, suffered Distress of their Goods for refusing to pay towar the Repairs of the Steeple-house there.

Anno 1690.

We shall close our Account of the Sufferings in this Count with a Collection of the Values of Corn and other Things, take out of the Fields from seventy Persons, for Tithes from the Yea 1681 to the Year 1690 inclusive, *viz.* :—359*l.* 16*s.* 5*d.*

[There is a lengthy account of the trial of *James Naylor* at th Sessions, held at Appleby, January, 1652, but not being a West morland Friend, it has been omitted].

PRINTED BY STEEL BROTHERS, CARLISLE.

CPSIA information can be obtained
at www.ICGtesting.com
Printed in the USA
LVHW101550090223
738797LV00035B/181

9 783382 100339